Samuel Robinson

Sketch of the Life and Writings of Ferdusi

a Persian poet who flourished in the 10th century

Samuel Robinson

Sketch of the Life and Writings of Ferdusi
a Persian poet who flourished in the 10th century

ISBN/EAN: 9783337293659

Printed in Europe, USA, Canada, Australia, Japan

Cover: Foto ©Andreas Hilbeck / pixelio.de

More available books at **www.hansebooks.com**

SKETCH OF THE LIFE AND

WRITINGS OF FERDUSI,

*A Persian Poet who flourished in the
10th Century.*

" PRAISE BE TO THE SOUL OF FERDUSI; THAT BLESSED
AND HAPPILY-ENDOWED NATURE!
"HE WAS NOT OUR TEACHER AND WE HIS DISCIPLES;
HE WAS OUR LORD AND WE HIS SLAVES."—*Unsari.*

LONDON :
PUBLISHED BY WILLIAMS & NORGATE,
HENRIETTA STREET, COVENT GARDEN;
AND BY JAMES CORNISH, MANCHESTER.

MDCCCLXXVI.

ADVERTISEMENT.

It may be proper to state, that the substance of the following little volume is a Paper which was read now many years ago in 1823, before the Literary and Philosophical Society of Manchester, and is printed in their Transactions. It is now reprinted with the passages originally selected newly translated and re-arranged, and with additional specimens of Ferdusi's Shah-Namah; in the same size and form as Specimens of several other distinguished Persian Poets by the same translator, of which a list is given at the end of the volume.

S. R.

Wilmslow, 1876.

TABLE OF CONTENTS.

———∞∞❉∞∞———

List of Specimens by the same Translator at the end.

THE LIFE AND WRITINGS OF FERDUSI.

§ 1st.—*The Life of Ferdusi.*

Ferdusi was born at Tûs, a town of Khorasan, **a** province of Persia, about the middle of the tenth century of our era. He was of respectable parentage, his father being a gardener; some say in the service of the Governor. His father, according to the legend, had a dream, which made him consult a celebrated interpreter of dreams, who told him that his son would be a great scholar, whose fame would reach the four quarters of the earth. This encouraged him to give his son every advantage of education which he could afford, and the child seconded his efforts by early showing extraordinary talents and making rapid advances in literature, learning, and

poetry. His ardent love of knowledge is said to
have attracted the attention of the poet Assadi, who
assisted him in his studies, and encouraged his rising
genius ; and to whose instructions he probably owed
his taste for poetry, and that intimate acquaintance
with history, which led him afterwards to employ his
muse in dignifying and embellishing the popular
traditions of his country. At this period India was
governed by the celebrated Mahmûd, of Ghazni. The
poets whom he favoured have sung his praises, and
ascribed to him the possession of every virtue. He
was certainly, at all events, a warm patron of
literature ; and learned and ingenious men found a
flattering reception at his Court. His chief amuse-
ments were poetry and history. Considerable
collections had been made by several of the former
monarchs of Persia of such legends and historical
documents as seemed the most authentic ; and in the
reign of Yezdejerd the last King of the dynasty,
before the Persian Empire was finally conquered and
overthrown by the Mohammedans, that sovereign had
assembled the learned Mubids, or Priests of the
Fire-Worshippers, and commanded them to compose
from them a connected history of the country from
the reign of the first King Kaiumeras to that of
Khosru-Parviz, his immediate predecessor. This volume

on the defeat of Yezdejerd is said to have been sent
to the Khalif Omar, who at first intended to have it
translated, but, finding it to consist of what he
deemed fictitious and immoral topics, abandoned the
idea. The book was afterwards presented, it is
added, to the King of Abyssinia, who had copies
made of it, and distributed through the East, and so
preserved it from destruction. This part of the
account, however, in itself very improbable, needs
confirmation.

The Vizier of Yakub-ben Laith, about A.H. 260,
A.D. 837, by order of his Sovereign, called together
the most learned Mubids, and with their assistance,
and by the offers of valuable rewards to every one
who would send him records or documents, formed
from them a complete history of Persia down to the
death of Yezdejerd.

Mahmûd had considerably added to these collections, and it was his wish to possess a series of heroic
poems composed from these materials. This appears
to have been a favourite idea with some of the ancient
Persian monarchs.

The poet Dukiki was employed for this purpose by
one of the Princes of the race of Sassan ; or, as some
say, for the accounts vary, of the family of Saman ;
but he dying by the hand of a slave after having

written only two thousand verses, the design had been abandoned. It was afterwards resumed by Mahmûd, who wished to add another glory to his reign by procuring the completion of this great work under his own auspices, and he accordingly entertained several poets at his Court with this intention.

Ferdusi, conscious of his genius, was inspired with an ardent desire of enjoying the reputation which would necessarily follow the successful accomplishment of so bold but glorious an undertaking. He communicated his plan to his friends at Tûs, and, encouraged by them, composed an heroic poem on the delivery of Persia by Feridun from the tyranny of Zohak. This production was received with universal applause, and introduced the poet to Abu Mansar, Governor of Tûs, who urged him to proceed with ardour in the noble career on which he had entered, and gave him flattering assurances of success. Ferdusi has gratefully owned his obligations to him, and has elegantly sung his praises at the commencement of his poem.

Confident of his strength, Ferdusi now determined to repair to Ghazni, as to a proper theatre for the display of his genius, and the acquisition of that fame which he felt that he was destined one day to enjoy. As the story is told by Jami in his Baharistan, entering the city as a stranger, he saw three persons sitting in a garden, to whom he offered his salutations. These proved to be Ansari, Farrakhi, and Asjadi, three of the Court poets, who, when they saw Ferdusi enter and approach them, unwilling to admit him into their society, agreed to repeat each a verse of a tetrastick, and to require the stranger to supply a fourth rhyme, fancying that there was no fourth rhyme in the language, before they would allow him to do so. They accordingly recited each of them one of the following lines :—

> The moon's mild radiance thy soft looks disclose,
> Thy blooming cheeks might shame the virgin rose ;
> Thine eye's dark glance the cuirass pierces through,

To which Ferdusi immediately replied—

> Like Poshun's javelin in the fight with Gu.

To add to their mortification, the poets were obliged to confess their ignorance of the story to which he alluded, and which he narrated to them at length. (*Note* 1.)

He soon established himself in the favour of Mahmud, who allotted to him the honourable task of composing the work which he had projected. Every evening he read to the Sultan what he had written during the day, and Mahmûd was so much delighted with these specimens of his performance, that, on one occasion, he promised him a gold dinar for every verse which he should write, but Ferdusi declined receiving any reward till the whole should be finished.

At length, after the unremitted toil of thirty years, and in the seventieth year of his age, Ferdusi brought to a conclusion his immortal poem, and presented it to the Sultan. But either envy and malice had been too successfully employed in depreciating the value of his labours, or possibly mingled feelings of avarice and bigotry on the part of the monarch induced him to bestow upon the poet a reward very inadequate to his deserts.

According to another account, Hussain Maimandi, who, though not Vizier, as some writers have said, enjoyed much influence at Court, and who for some reason had become his personal enemy, changed the promised sum of gold dinars into silver ones. Ferdusi was in the bath when the money was brought to him. The high-minded poet could not brook the insult. He divided the paltry present between the boy who bore it, the servant of the bath, and a vendor of sherbets, and, retiring to his closet, wrote an animated invective against the Sultan, of which the following is a specimen:—

Many kings have there been before thee,
Who were all crowned with the sovereignty of the
    world,
More exalted than thou in rank,
Richer in treasures and armies, and thrones, and
    diadems ;
But their acts were those only of justice and good-
    ness,
They concerned themselves not about saving and
    spending ;
They ruled with equity those under their hand,
And were pure and pious worshippers of God ;
They sought from the future only a good name,
And seeking a good name found a happy ending :
But those who are bound in the fetters of avarice
Will be contemptible in the judgment of the wise.

Thou wouldest not look upon this my Book,
Thou turnedst away to speak evil words of me ;
But whoever esteemeth my poetry lightly,
Him will the circling heavens hardly regard with
    favour.
I have put forth this chronicle of Kings,
Written in mine own beautiful language,
And when I have come nigh my seventieth year
My hopes at one stroke have become as the wind.

Thirty years long in this transitory inn
I have toiled laboriously in the hope of my reward,
And completed a work of sixty thousand couplets,
Finished with the beauty and skill of the master ;
Describing the deeds and weapons of war,
And plains, and oceans, and deserts, and rivers,
And wild beasts, and dragons, and monstrous giants,
And the sorceries of man-wolves, and enchantments
        of demons,
Whose yells and howlings reach the heavens ;
And men of mark in the day of the fight,
And heroic warriors on the field of battle,
And men distinguished for their rank and actions,
As Feridun, and Afrasiab, and the brazen-faced
        Rustam,
And Tahmuras, the powerful binder of demons,
And Manucheher, and Jamshid, the lofty monarch,
And Dara, and Sikandar, the King of Kings,
And Kai-Khosru, who wore the imperial crown,
And Kai-Kaus, Nushirvan, and a crowd of others,
Champions in the tournament, and lions in the battle,
Men who all lay dead in the lapse of ages,
And to whose names my writings have given a new
        life.

I lived, O king, a life of slavery
In order to leave some memorial of thee.

The pleasant dwelling may become a ruin,
Through the force of the rain and the blazing sun.
I nourished the desire of building in my verses
A lofty palace which would defy destruction from
      wind and rain,
And pass through generations in this chronicle,
Which every man of intelligence would read:
But of this thou broughtest me no good tidings,
And the King of the earth gave me not a hope.

During these thirty years I bore many anxieties,
And in my Persian have restored Persia to life:
And hadest thou, Ruler of the earth, not had the
      niggardly hand,
Thou wouldest have led me to the place of honour,
And had intelligence come to the aid of the king,
Thou wouldest have seated me on a throne.
But when he who wears the diadem is not of noble
      birth,
He amongst crowned heads will receive no mention.

Hadest thou, O King, been the son of a King,
Thou wouldest have placed on my head a golden
      crown ;
Had thy mother been a lady of royal birth,
Thou wouldest have heaped up gold and silver to my
      knees ;

But he whose tribe can shew no great man,
Ought not to bear the name of the great.

When I had worked painfully on this Book of Kings
    for thirty years,
That the King might give me a reward from his
    treasury,
That he might raise me to independence amongst the
    people,
That he might exalt me amongst the nobles,
He opened the door of his treasure-house, and gave
    me,
My sole reward—a cup of barley-water :
With the price of a cup of barley-water from the
    king's treasury
I bought me a draught of barley-water in the street.

The vilest of things is better than such a king,
Who possesseth neither honour, nor piety, nor morals !
But the son of a slave will never do aught of good,
Though he should be father of a line of kings :
For to exalt the head of the unworthy,
To look for anything of good from them,
Is to lose the thread which guideth your purpose,
And to nourish a serpent in your bosom.

The tree which is by nature bitter,
Though thou shouldest plant it in the garden of
    Paradise,
And spread honey about its roots—yea the purest
    honey-comb,
And water it in its season from the fountain of
    Eternity,
Would in the end betray its nature,
And would still produce bitter fruit.
If thou shouldest pass through the shop of the seller
    of amber,
Thy garments will retain its odour ;
If thou shouldest enter the forge of the blacksmith,
Thou wilt there see nothing but blackness ;
That evil should come of an evil disposition is no
    wonder.
For thou canst not sponge out the darkness from the
    night ;
Of the son of the impure man entertain no hope,
For the Ethiopian by washing will never become
    white.
From the evil-eye expect no good,
It is only to cast the dust into thine own.

Yet had the king had regard to his reputation,
He would have deemed it a precious thing to tread
    the way of knowledge ;

In the institutes of the Kings and in the old customs
Thou wouldest have found maxims such as these;
Thou wouldest have looked on my longings with
    another eye,
Thou wouldest not thus utterly have ruined my
    fortunes.
For to this end I composed my lofty verses,
That the King might draw from them lessons of
    wisdom;
That he might learn what it would be well to treasure
    in his thoughts
Of the words and counsels of the aged wise man;
And that never should he dare to injure the poet,
Nor even regard him with less than reverence :
For the poet, when grieved, will speak out his satire,
And his satire will endure to the day of resurrection.

O King Mahmûd, conqueror of kingdoms,
If thou fearest not man, at least fear God,
For to the court of the Holy-one will I carry my
    complaint,
Bowing down and scattering dust upon my head.

    In flying from Ghazni to escape from the indigna-
tion of Mahmûd, Ferdusi passed through Kohistan,
where he was kindly received by Nasir-ud-din
Mohtashm, its Governor. Mohtashm had personal

obligations to Mahmûd, and finding afterwards that
Ferdusi proposed to publish other writings reflecting
on the conduct of the Sultan, he besought him to
forego his intention, bestowing upon him at the same
time a considerable sum of money. To this request
Ferdusi acceded in the following verses :—

Although I was lacerated to the heart, my friend,
By the injustice of that iniquitous King,
For he had blighted the labour of thirty years,
And my complaint had ascended from earth to heaven;
And though I had purposed to publish my complaint,
And to spread the tale of his conduct throughout the
    world;
And though I could have spoken with scorn of his
    father and his mother,
For I tremble at nothing save the Throne of God;
And though I could have so blackened his reputation,
That no water would ever have washed out the stain;
And, since he hath changed from friend to enemy,
Would have laid him bare with the scalpel of my
    tongue;
Yet, Mohtashm, thou hast commanded,
And I know not how I can withdraw my head from
    thy command:
Therefore have I sent thee all that I still have by me
    of my writings,

Nothing have I withholden, or kept back for myself.
If there be aught improper in the writings,
Burn them with fire, wash them out with water ;
For myself, O generous Prince,
I appeal from this to that Higher Court,
Where God will listen in mercy to my plea,
And at whose judgment-seat I shall receive justice.

From Kohistan Ferdusi proceeded to Mazinderan, where he spent some time at the court of a prince of that country, occupied principally in the revisal and correction of his great work. Still, however, apprehensive of the effects of the Sultan's displeasure, he quitted this place to take refuge at Baghdad, where, as soon as he had made himself known, he was received with great distinction by Kader Billah Abassi, the reigning Khaliph, at whose court he resided some time in tolerable tranquillity. But the fury of Mahmûd still pursued him. He wrote to the Khaliph to demand Ferdusi, threatening, in case of a refusal, to lead an army against him. The generous prince, unwilling to give up the man who had sought his protection, and unable to meet the Sultan in the field, was reluctantly obliged to dismiss him. He wrote to Mahmûd, to inform him that Ferdusi had withdrawn himself from his protection ; and, bestow-

ing on the illustrious wanderer a considerable sum
of money, advised him to seek an asylum with the
princes of Yaman. To Tûs, however, his native
place, not to Yaman, did the poet proceed, where he
died, at an advanced age, about the year 1021 of our
era.

It is added that Mahmûd, afterwards relenting in
his anger, or perhaps fearing that his conduct would
be viewed by posterity in a disgraceful light, sent the
stipulated present to Ferdusi, with a conciliatory
letter; that it arrived on the very day Ferdusi was
buried; but that his daughter, to whom it was
offered, refused it, saying that she would not accept
what had been denied to her father. Nasir Khosru,
however, in proof that some gift was at last
sent, relates in his Saffernamah, or Book of
Travels, that when he was at Tûs, in the year 437
of the Hajira (A.D. 1045), he saw a splendid public
edifice, newly erected, and was informed that it was
built by order of Mahmûd, with the money which
the daughter of the poet had refused.

It is proper to state that some of the circumstances
mentioned in the preceding narrative are taken from
a MS. account of the life of Ferdusi, which is pre-
fixed to almost all the copies of his works. It forms

a part of the preface to the corrected edition of the
Shah-namah, made by the order of Bayasanghar
Khan, one of the descendants of the Emperor Timur,
and published in the year of the Hajira 829 (A.D.
1425-6), and may be supposed, therefore, to contain
all that was then known of the poet; but it is the
only detailed account of his life which we have, and as
we possess few means of testing its perfect authen-
ticity; and as few Oriental Biographies, especially of
their ancient authors, are written in a critical spirit,
or with care or discrimination, with regard to the collection and verification of the facts narrated, we can
never place implicit reliance on their correctness.
Ferdusi, however, was so illustrious a character, and
his connection with Mahmûd procured him so much
notoriety, that probably the main circumstances of
his life may be accepted as having been recorded with
tolerable truthfulness.

§ 2nd.—*Character of Ferdusi's Writings.*

Eight hundred years have now elapsed since the publication of Ferdusi's great work, and it still continues to receive in the East that admiration with which it was hailed on its first appearance. Whatever, indeed, be the opinion which European readers may form of it, the Shah-namah is confessedly the noblest production of Persian genius; and the applause which has been bestowed upon it by some liberal and enlightened critics of the Western world may incline us to believe that all its merit does not depend upon mere Oriental prejudices. The assertion, indeed, that all the literary productions of the East are a tissue of absurd fictions and ideas, written in a barbarous and bombastic style, with few marks of adherence to truth and nature, is much too loose and general, and proceeds oftentimes from ignorance, or from false

principles of judgment.   This is not a suitable place
for instituting an inquiry into the reality of the
existence of a fixed standard of taste, which the
varying conclusions of different writers on the subject
might almost lead us to suspect ; it may not, however,
be improper to observe, that the manners, customs,
and opinions of every nation necessarily impart a
peculiar character to its literary productions, and
that they ought not to be tried without a reference
to those customs and opinions.   We may read the
classical poets, and enjoy their mythology and ideas,
and yet be disgusted with the modern poet, who, on
the sanction of classical usage, presents to us the
same assembly of the Gods, still controlling mortal
events.   We may sympathise with the despairing
Roman, who invokes a Goddess, in whom he believes,
to favour his passion, but shall accuse of affectation
and coldness the modern poet, who addresses his
vows to the same divinity.   To relish thoroughly,
therefore, the literature of any nation we shall have
to imbue ourselves with something of the spirit in
which it was conceived, and familiarize ourselves
with the prevailing ideas of the times which gave it
birth.   If we do this with regard to the works of
Oriental writers, we may find in them, amidst many
extravagant notions and false thoughts, not a few

also calculated to delight the fancy and fill the mind
with pleasing images. Why should we disdain to
receive from the Persian fictions of a Ferdusi· something of the pleasure which we derive from the
Medieval beliefs of a Tasso, or the Scottish super-
stitions of a Burns or a Collins?

The SHAH-NAMAH, or BOOK OF KINGS, is usually
said to have contained 60,000 couplets, or 120,000
lines.—(*Note 2.*) It has been called by some an epic
poem, by others a series of epic poems; but neither
with much propriety. It is in truth merely a Historical poem, similar in many respects to our ancient
rhyming chronicles, but highly embellished with all
the ornaments of poetry and fable. It embraces the
whole period of ancient Persian history, commencing
with the reign of Kaiumeras, the first king, and
ending with that of Yezdejerd, the monarch who
governed Persia when that country was invaded and
subjugated by the Arabs. Reign follows reign with
undeviating exactness; the natural order of events is
rarely disturbed; nor are the incidents of the poem
made conducive to the development of one great
action, or to the inculcation of any grand moral truth.
Sometimes, indeed, we may perceive a kind of action
complete within itself, but we may generally trace it
rather to the unity of some great historical event in

itself, than to the design of the poet. As a work of art, therefore, the Shah-namah is certainly defective; and it is unjust, in endeavouring to estimate its merits, to bring it into comparison with the more regular and classical models of European invention. We might, indeed, liken it to the Orlando Furioso of Ariosto, to which it bears a considerable resemblance in several respects; particularly in the irregularities of its structure, the wildness of its incidents, and the neglect of strict method which characterizes the muse of that poet. Nor ought we to be so unreasonable as to condemn a performance because it is not written precisely on the plan which we should most have desired. It is sufficient to establish the excellence of a work that the author has done well what under the circumstances it was in his power to do. The plan of Ferdusi was chalked out for him; and every one who has read any considerable portion of the Shah-namah must be delighted at the admirable manner in which he has executed the difficult task imposed upon him.

In taking a view of the genius of Ferdusi as a poet, the object which first strikes us is his amazing power of invention. The materials from which he composed the historical part of his work have unfortunately perished, so that we cannot exactly determine to what extent he enjoyed this power; but that he possessed it in an extraordinary degree no one who is conversant with his writings can for a moment doubt. The records with which he was furnished consisted, most probably, only of dry facts or fabulous legends. He might draw many of his stories, and the names of some of his principal heroes, from the popular traditions of his country, but the form and character which he has given to the whole must be considered to be the fruit of his own creative genius. On a very narrow basis he has founded a structure, irregular indeed in its design, and unequal in its execution, but of so vast proportions, and, in particular parts, so highly finished, that we cannot contemplate it without sentiments of astonishment and admiration. He has skilfully interwoven into his poem the whole range of Persian enchantment and fable, and has at the same time enlivened his narrative with so many agreeable episodes and adventures, that the attention of the reader is constantly diverted, and he is led on, generally without weariness or effort, through the pages of this stupendous performance. Whoever, indeed, considers the immense length of the work, the copiousness of the subject, and the variety which reigns throughout it, cannot fail to have a high opinion of the exuberance of the poet's fancy, and the uncommon fertility of his ideas.

The originality of Ferdusi is scarcely to be questioned. .He had no one before him from whom to copy, and his excellences are, therefore, wholly his own. His conceptions are in general lively and vigorous ; his thoughts bold and forcible ; his descriptions and narratives striking and animated. Everywhere, throughout his poem, we feel the glow of a rich and ardent imagination. Ferdusi has made but little use of mythology. Events are generally brought about without the intervention of superhuman agency ; but the extraordinary qualities with which the poet invests some of his heroes, as it places us in a manner among another race of beings, may render the use of machinery an object of less importance.

The minute and perfect delineation of character is rarely the distinguishing excellence of very early poets. In a nation emerging out of barbarism, the characters of men are in general sufficiently original and poetical, but they must be viewed in classes rather than as individuals. Those slighter traits which distinguish one individual from another of the same class can be called into existence only with the progress of refinement, or are too evanescent to be observed till men begin to be brought into closer contact by the influence of society. Homer, great as he is in this respect, is inferior to Tasso in the fine discrimination of characters marked by the same general qualities. Ferdusi is still inferiour to Homer. Yet the characters of the Shah-namah are, on the whole, well supported, and varied and contrasted with considerable skill and there are a few which are touched with a delicacy and beauty hardly to have been expected in a poet of his age and country.

The descriptions of Ferdusi are rich and tolerably varied, and it is in the descriptive parts of his poem that he will probably be thought by many to have displayed his happiest talent. Born in the favoured country of fiction and romance; familiar from an ear y period of his life with the magnificence of the most powerful and splendid court of Asia; it is not to be doubted that his mind must have been early impressed with scenes and stories, and imbued with associations, admirably calculated to make a deep impression on a naturally ardent and lively imagination. His battles are painted in bold and lively colours; and when we read of pomps and processions, and royal banquets, and gardens and palaces, adorned with everything which wealth and power united can command, we have little difficulty in following the poet in his loftier flights, and are scarcely disposed to criticise them as too bold, or the language in which they are conveyed as too luxuriant. His narratives

are generally spirited and poetical. His sentiments
just and noble. His touches of real passion often
appeal forcibly to the heart, and convince us that the
poet felt the emotions which he describes. The
dignity and beauty of the moral reflections, which
are liberally scattered throughout the work, would
alone render it highly valuable. The following fine
passage may be selected as an example :—

One thou exaltest, and givest him dominion,
Another thou castest as food to the fishes;
One thou enrichest with treasure like Karûn,
Another thou feedest with the bread of affliction.
Nor is that a proof of thy love, nor this of thy hatred,
For thou, the Creator of the world, knowest what is fit ;
Thou assignest to each man his high or low estate,
And how shall I describe thee ?—THOU ART WHAT THOU ART!

We find in his poems many touches of tenderness
and pathos, such as : —

Crush not yon emmet, as it drageth along its grain,
For it hath life, and its sweet life is pleasant to it.

Or, as Sir William Jones renders it :—

Crush not yond emmet, rich in hoarded grain ;
It lives with pleasure, and it dies with pain.

For which Sadi, who cites it in the Bostan, invokes
blessings on his departed spirit.

The diction of Ferdusi is soft and elegant, but at
the same time lively and animated. His versification
smooth and polished. His style easy and natural.
The Shah-namah is written in the purest dialect of

the old Persian, before it had received much admix-
ture of Arabic words. Mohammed, who admired it
for its extreme sweetness, used to declare that it would
be the language of Paradise.

Ferdusi is distinguished from all other Persian
poets by that simplicity which is almost always the
accompaniment of the highest order of genuis. In
thus speaking of his simplicity, it is not to be
understood that many instances of bad taste and
exaggeration may not be found in his writings, but
still they show a wonderful freedom from those mere-
tricious ornaments, puerile conceits, and affected
forms of expression, which disgrace the best compositions of his countrymen.

It does not consist with the object of the present
sketch to enter into a critical detail of the faults of
Ferdusi. The Shah-namah—admirable as it is in
many respects—is still a Persian poem, and the can-
dour of European critics must be called upon to make
large allowances for its imperfections. In so long a
performance it is not wonderful that there are passages which are tedious, and that the action sometimes languishes. The minuteness of the poet sometimes degenerates into feebleness, and occasionally
becomes ridiculous. He has many weak and faulty
verses. His figures are sometimes too gigantic or

far-fetched; his thoughts sometimes forced and unnatural. His language occasionally is too inflated, and sometimes borders on extravagance. But these and other blemishes may be traced rather to the age and country in which he lived than to any defect of genius. "Had he been born in Europe," says the laborious editor of the first printed edition of the Shah-namah, "he might have left a work more to our taste; but, born anywhere, he could not fail to impress on his writings the stamp and character of his extraordinary powers. These are accordingly acknowledged and felt throughout the whole extent of the Mohammedan world, and will, I doubt not, be recognised in Europe, amidst all the vices of a Persian taste; with which, indeed, he is much less tinctured, in my opinion, than any Persian poet I have ever read."—(*Note* 3).

In fine, Ferdusi, in whatever light we contemplate him, was certainly a remarkable man; and if genius be estimated, not by the absolute height which it reaches in the scale of excellence, but by the degree to which it has risen by its own unassisted efforts, that of Ferdusi may be thought to rival that of some who have produced more finished works, amidst more favourable opportunities of approaching towards perfection. In the history of Persian literature, at least, the Shah-namah must ever be regarded as a distinguished object. It is a great storehouse whence succeeding poets have drawn their images and fables, and it has certainly had a very considerable influence on the literary productions of the country which gave it birth. Ferdusi has the rare merit of having identified himself with the feelings and associations of his countrymen. His poems still continue to form the delight of the Oriental world, and must endure as long as the language in which they are written. To such a man, in the strength of conscious genius, it may without much imputation of vanity be permitted to exclaim, as he has done at the conclusion of his great undertaking,—

When this famous book was brought to a conclusion,
The face of the earth was filled with my renown,
And every one who hath intelligence and wisdom and faith
After I am dead will shower praises upon me.
Henceforward I shall never die, for I have lived long enough
To scatter abroad the seeds of eloquence.—(*Note* 4.)

§ *3rd.—Specimens of Ferdusi's Poems.*

In selecting some specimens of Ferdusi's poetry, it has seemed advisable to the translator to chuse, in treating of a great heroic and narrative Poet, some portion in a sufficiently extended and connected form to exhibit his manner and power of telling a story, and to retain its dramatic character so far as to excite and sustain the interest of the auditor. For this purpose he has fixed upon the EPISODE of ZAL and RUDABAH, acknowledged to be one of the most beautiful portions of the Shah-namah. Other parts of the poem might, perhaps, furnish us with passages of greater sublimity and more varied description, but few or none are marked by more tenderness and feeling, or a deeper knowledge of human passions and affections: qualities which, as they are less frequently found in the compositions of Persia, render the genius of Ferdusi the more admirable. This Episode, moreover, possesses the advantage of a certain unity of subject, and plan, which renders it in some sort a short complete epic of itself. But to understand it better, it may be well to premise that Zâl is the son of Sâm Nariman, one of the Generals of Manuchahar, King of Persia. Having the misfortune to be born with white hair, he incurs the disgust of his father, who orders him to be exposed on the savage mountain of Elburz, where he is nurtured by the Simurgh, an immense fabulous vulture, which figures in the legends of Persia. After a time the affection of the parent is revived towards his child. He is recovered from the care of the Simurgh, and arrived at manhood is sent to govern the frontier province of Zabûl; the adjoining province of Kabûl, though tributary to the Persian empire, being governed by its own king, named Mihrab. The episode commences with a visit which Mihrab pays to Zâl. Zâl receives him with distinguished honour, entertains him at a sumptuous banquet, and they separate with mutual respect.

Then a chief of the great ones around him
Said:—O thou, the Hero of the world,
This Mihrab hath a daughter behind the veil,
Whose face is more resplendent than the sun;
From head to foot pure as ivory;
With a cheek like the spring, and in stature like the
    teak-tree.

Upon her silver shoulders descend two musky tresses,
Which, like nooses, fetter the captive;
Her lip is like the pomegranate, and her cheek like
　　　its flower;
Her eyes resemble the narcissus in the garden;
Her eyelashes have borrowed the blackness of the
　　　raven,
Her eyebrows are arched like a fringed bow.
Wouldest thou behold the mild radiance of the moon,
　　　look upon her countenance!
Wouldest thou inhale delightful odours, she is all
　　　fragrance!
She is altogether a paradise of sweets,
Decked with all grace, all music, all thou canst desire!
She would be fitting for thee, O warrior of the world,
She is as the heavens above to such as we are.—(*Note 5.*)

On hearing this description, Zâl becomes enamoured
of the fair unseen.

When Zâl heard this description,
His love leaped to the lovely maiden:
His heart boiled over with the heat of passion,
So that understanding and rest departed from him.
Night came, but he sat groaning, and buried in
　　　thought;
And a prey to sorrow for the not-yet-seen.

Mihrab pays a second visit to Zâl, and as he is returning his wife Sindocht and his daughter Rudabah espy him from a balcony, and stop him to make inquiries about the Hero.

O beautiful silver-bosomed cypress,
In the wide world not one of the Heroes
Will come up to the measure of Zâl.
In the pictured palace men will never behold the
      image
Of a warrior so strong, or so firm in the saddle.

He hath the heart of a lion, the power of an elephant,
And the strength of his arm is as the rush of the Nile.
When he sitteth on the throne he scattereth gold
      before him;
In the battle the heads of his enemies.

His cheek is ruddy as the flower of the arghavân;
Young in years, all alive, and the favourite of fortune,
And though his hair is white as though with age,
Yet in his bravery he could tear to pieces the water-
      serpent.

He rageth in the conflict with the fury of the crocodile,
He fighteth in the saddle like a sharp-fanged dragon.
In his wrath he staineth the earth with blood,
As he wieldeth his bright cimeter around him.

And though his hair is as white as is a fawn's,
In vain would the fault-finder seek another defect!
Nay! the whiteness of his hair even becometh him;
Thou wouldest say that he is born to beguile all
    hearts!

When Rudabah heard this description,
Her heart was set on fire, and her cheek crimsoned
    like the pomegranate.
Her whole soul was filled with the love of Zâl,
And food, and peace, and quietude were driven far
    from her.

After a time Rudabah resolves to reveal her passion
to her attendants.

Then she said to her prudent slaves,—
I will discover what I have hitherto concealed;
Ye are each of you the depositaries of my secrets,
My attendants, and the partners of my griefs.
I am agitated with love like the raging ocean,
Whose billows are heaved to the sky.
My once bright heart is filled with the love of Zâl,
My sleep is broken with thoughts of him;
My soul is perpetually filled with my passion,
Night and day my thoughts dwell upon his counte-
    nance.

Not one except yourselves knoweth my secret,
Ye—my affectionate and faithful servants,
What remedy now can ye devise for my case?
What will ye do for me? What promise will ye
     give me?
Some remedy ye must devise,
To free my heart and soul from this unhappiness.

Astonishment seized the slaves,
That dishonour should come nigh the daughter of
     kings;
In the anxiety of their hearts they started from their
     seats,
And all gave answer with one voice:—
O crown of the ladies of the earth,
Maiden pre-eminent amongst the pre-eminent,
Whose praise is spread abroad from Hindustan to
     China,
The resplendent ring in the circle of the Haram;
Whose stature surpasseth every cypress in the garden;
Whose cheek rivaleth the lustre of the Pleiades;
Whose picture is sent by the ruler of Kanûj
Even to the distant Monarchs of the West;
Have you ceased to be modest in your own eyes?
Have you lost all reverence for your father?
That whom his own parent cast from his bosom,

Him you will receive into your's ?
A man who was nurtured by a bird in the mountains !
A man who was a bye-word amongst the people !
  You—with your roseate countenance and musky
      tresses—
Seek a man whose hair is already white with age !
You—who have filled the world with admiration,
Whose portrait hangeth in every palace,
And whose beauty, and ringlets, and stature are such
That you might draw down a husband from the skies !

  To this remonstrance she makes the following
indignant answer :—

When Rudabah heard their reply,
Her heart blazed up like fire before the wind.
She raised her voice in anger against them,
Her face flushed, but she cast down her eyes.
After a time, grief and anger mingled in her coun-
      tenance,
And knitting her brows with passion, she exclaimed—
O, unadvised and worthless counsellors,
It was not becoming in me to ask your advice !
Were my eye dazzled by a star,
How could it rejoice to gaze even upon the moon ?
He who is formed of worthless clay will not regard
      the rose,

Although the rose is in nature more estimable than
　　clay!
I wish not for Cæsar, nor Emperor of China,—
　　　　　　　　　　　　　　　　(*Note* 6).
Nor for any one of the tiara-crowned Monarchs of
　　Irân;
The son of Sâm, Zâl, alone is my equal,
With his lion-like limbs, and arms, and shoulders.
You may call him as you please, an old man, or a
　　young,
To me he is in the room of heart and of soul.
Except him never shall anyone have a place in my
　　heart;
Mention not to me any one except him.
Him hath my love chosen unseen,
Yea, hath chosen him only from description.
For him is my affection, not for face or hair,
And I have sought his love in the way of honour.

Her vehemence overcomes the reluctance of the
slaves, and one of them promises, if possible, to contrive an interview.

May hundreds of thousands such as we are be a
　　sacrifice for thee;
May the wisdom of the creation be thy worthy
　　portion;

May thy dark narcissus-eye be ever full of modesty ;
May thy cheek be ever tinged with bashfulness.
If it be necessary to learn the art of the magician,
To sow-up the eyes with the bands of enchantment,
We will fly till we surpass the enchanter's bird,
We will run like the deer in search of a remedy ;
Perchance we may draw the king nigh unto his moon,
And place him securely at thy side.

The vermil lip of Rudabah was filled with smiles ;
She turned her saffron-tinged countenance toward the
        slave, and said,
If thou shalt bring this matter to a happy issue,
Thou hast planted for thyself a stately and fruitful
        tree,
Which every day shall bear rubies for its fruit,
And shall pour that fruit into thy lap.

    The story proceeds to say, how the slaves fulfil
their promise. They go forth, and find Zâl prac-
ticing with the bow. Busying themselves in gathering
roses, they attract his attention. He shoots an arrow
in that direction, and sends his quiver-bearer to bring
it back. The slaves inquire who the Hero is who
draws the bow with so much strength and skill. The
boy answers scornfully,—"Do they not know that
it is Zâl, the most renowned warrior in the world."

In reply, they vaunt the superiour attractions of
Rudabah. The boy reports their account of her to
Zâl, who goes to speak to them, receives from them
a warm description of her charms, and presses them
to procure for him the means of obtaining an interview. This little incident is well-imagined: it is
Zâl who is made to ask for the meeting, and the
honour of Rudabah is not compromised. The slaves
return to their mistress and report upon their mission,
eulogizing the goodly qualities of the Hero. Her
ironical answer to their former depreciation is animated and natural.

Then said the elegant cypress-formed lady to her
       maidens,—
Other than this were once your words and your
       counsel !
Is this then the Zâl, the nursling of a bird?
This the old-man, white-haired and withered?
Now his cheek is ruddy as the flower of the arghavân;
His stature is tall, his face beautiful, his presence
       lordly !
Ye have exalted my charms before him;
Ye have spoken, and made me a bargain !
She said, and her lips were full of smiles;
But her cheek crimsoned like the bloom of pome-
       granate.

The interview takes place in a private pavilion of
the Princess; and the account of it is marked with
more than one touch of truth and beauty.

When from a distance the son of the valiant Sâm,
Became visible to the illustrious maiden,
She opened her gem-like lips, and exclaimed,
Welcome, thou brave and happy youth!
The blessing of the Creator of the world be upon thee!
On him who is the father of a son like thee!
May Destiny ever favour thy wishes!
May the vault of heaven be the ground thou walkest
     on!
The dark night is turned into day by thy countenance,
The world is soul-enlivened by the fragrance of thy
     presence!
Thou hast travelled hither on foot from thy palace,
Thou hast pained to behold me thy royal footsteps!

When the Hero heard the voice from the battlement,
He looked up and beheld a face resplendent as the sun,
Irradiating the terrace like a flashing jewel,
And brightening the ground like a flaming ruby.

Then he replied,—O thou who sheddest the mild
     radiance of the moon,
The blessing of Heaven, and mine be upon thee!

How many nights hath cold Arcturus beholden me
Uttering my cry to God, the Pure,
And beseeching the Lord of the universe,
That he would vouchsafe to unveil thy countenance
　　　before me !
Now I am made joyful in hearing thy voice,
In listening to thy rich and gracious accents.
But seek, I pray thee, some way to thy presence,
For what converse can we hold, I on the ground, and
　　　thou on the terrace ?

The Peri-faced maiden heard the words of the Hero,
Quickly she unbound her auburn locks,
Coil upon coil, and serpent on serpent ;
And she stooped and dropped down the tresses from
　　　the battlement,
And cried, O Hero, child of Heroes,
Take now these tresses, they belong to thee,
And I have cherished them that they might prove an
　　　aid to my beloved.

And Zâl gazed upward at the lovely maiden,
And stood amazed at the beauty of her hair and of
　　　her countenance ;
He covered the musky ringlets with his kisses,
And his bride heard the kisses from above.
Then he exclaimed,—That would not be right !

May the bright sun never shine on such a day !
It were to lay my hand on the life of one already
   distracted ;
It were to plunge the arrow-point into my own
   wounded bosom.
Then he took his noose from his boy, and made a
   running knot,
And threw it, and caught it on the battlement,
And held his breath, and at one bound
Sprang from the ground, and reached the summit.

As soon as the Hero stood upon the terrace,
The Peri-faced maiden ran to greet him,
And took the hand of the Hero in her own,
And they went like those who are overcome with
   wine.

Then he descended from the lofty gallery,
His hand in the hand of the tall Princess,
And came to the door of the gold-painted pavilion,
And entered that royal assembly,
Which blazed with light like the bowers of Paradise ;
And the slaves stood like houries before them :
And Zâl gazed in astonishment,
On her face, and her hair, and her stately form, and
   on all that splendour.

And Zâl was seated in royal pomp
Opposite that mildly-radiant beauty;
And Rudabah could not rest from looking towards
      him,
And gazing upon him with all her eyes;
On that arm, and shoulder, and that splendid figure,
On the brightness of that soul-enlightening counte-
      nance;
So that the more and more she looked
The more and more was her heart inflamed.

Then he kissed and embraced her, renewing his
      vows,—
Can the lion help pursuing the wild ass?—
And said,— O sweet and graceful silver-bosomed
      maiden,
It may not be, that, both of noble lineage,
We should do aught unbecoming our birth;
For from Sâm Nariman I received an admonition,
To do no unworthy deed, lest evil should come of it;
For better is the seemly than the unseemly,
That which is lawful than that which is forbidden.
And I fear that Manuchahar, when he shall hear of
      this affair,
Will not be inclined to give it his approval;
I fear too that Sâm will exclaim against it,

And will boil over with passion, and lay his hand
    upon me.
Yet, though soul and body are precious to all men,
Life I will resign, and clothe myself with a shroud,—
And this I swear by the righteous God,—
Ere I will break the faith which I have pledged thee.
I will bow myself before Him, and offer my adoration,
And supplicate Him as those who worship Him in
    truth,
That he will cleanse the heart of Sâm, King of the
    earth,
From opposition, and rage, and rancour.
Perhaps the Creator of the world may listen to my
    prayer,
And thou mayest yet be publicly proclaimed my wife."

And Rudabah said,—And I also, in the presence of
    the righteous God,
Take the same pledge, and swear to thee my faith;
And He who created the world be witness to my words,
That no one but the Hero of the world,
The throned, the crowned, the far-famed Zâl,
Will I ever permit to be sovereign over me."

So their love every moment became greater;
Prudence was afar, and passion was predominant,

Till the grey dawn began to show itself,
And the drum to be heard from the royal pavilion.
Then Zâl bade adieu to the fair one;
His soul was darkened, and his bosom on fire;
And the eyes of both were filled with tears,
And they lifted up their voices against the sun;
"O glory of the universe, why come so quick?
Couldest thou not wait one little moment?"

Then Zâl cast his noose on a pinnacle,
And descended from those happy battlements,
As the sun was rising redly above the mountains,
And the bands of warriors were gathering in their
    ranks.

On returning to the camp Zâl assembles his counsellors, and consults them as to what he should do. They advise him to write to his father, and be guided by him. Zâl accordingly writes to Sâm. In his letter he recalls to him in an affecting manner all the sufferings he had endured when abandoned by his parents in the mountains, conjures him to consent to his union with Rudabah, and reminds him of his promise, when reclaiming him from the Simurgh, that in all the future circumstances of his life he would endeavour to efface the remembrance of his cruelty by a cheerful compliance with his wishes. Sâm is greatly embarrassed by this letter. On the one hand he fears the reproaches of his son, on the other the anger of the King. He convenes the sages, and bids them declare what will be the result of the union. After the intense study of many days they prophecy the birth of the famous Rustam.

The Astrologers came to Sâm Nariman and said,
O Warrior of the Golden Belt,
Joy will be to thee from the union of Zâl and of the
      daughter of Mihrab,
For they are two fortune-favoured equals,
And from them shall be born a hero, in strength an
      elephant,
Who shall gird his loins in manliness ;
Who shall bear dominion on his sword,   ✳
And shall exalt the throne of the King above the
      clouds.
The evil-minded he will cut off from the land,
Nor shall there remain a den on the face of the earth.
He will leave neither monster nor Demon of Mazin-
      deran,
And will sweep the earth with his mighty mace.
From him shall come many woes on Turan,
And Iran shall enjoy all happiness.
He will lull to sleep the head of the sufferer,

And will close the door of sorrow, and the path of
    calamity.
The hope of the Iranians shall be in him,
And in him the joy and confidence of the warrior.
His courser will bear the Hero proudly in the battle,
And he will bruise the faces of the tigers of war;
And the furious elephants and the fierce lions
Shall be annihilated beneath the club of the Hero;
And the monarchs of Hindustan, and Rûm, and Irân
Will engrave his name on their seals.
Fortunate will be the king in whose time
His renown will exalt the royal dignity."

On hearing this prophecy of the future greatness
of his grandson, Sâm is reconciled to the marriage,
but writes to Zâl to withhold the celebration of it
until he has been to the court of Manuchahar, and
obtained the sanction of the King. Zâl, transported
with joy, immediately sends the letter to Rudabah.
The messenger on her return is espied by her mother,
and the secret correspondence of the lovers is dis-
covered. The interview which follows between
Sindocht and her daughter is thus described:—

Then, greatly troubled, she entered the palace,
Full of pain, and anxiety, and sorrow;
She closed upon herself the door of her chamber,

And was as one distracted by the tumult of her
 thoughts.
She commanded her daughter to appear before her;
And she tore her cheeks with her hand,
And she watered their roses with her tearful eyes,
Till they became inflamed like the crimson rose.
She said to Rudabah,—O precious girl,
Why hast thou placed thyself on the brink of a
 precipice?
What is there left worth having in the world,
Which I have not showed to thee openly and in private?
Why, my beauty, hast thou become so unjust to me?
Tell, I beseech thee, all thy secrets to thy mother!
Who is this woman, and whence doth she come,
And what is the purpose for which she cometh to thee?
What is the meaning of this message? And who is
 the man
For whom is intended this ring, and this beautiful
 turban?

Rudabah looked down to her feet and the ground;
She stood abashed in the presence of her mother;
The tear of affection gushed from her eyes,
And her cheeks were crimsoned with the burning
 drops.
Then she said to her mother,—O full of wisdom,

Love is chasing my soul before it.
Would that my mother had never given me birth!
That neither good nor evil had been uttered concern-
        ing me!
The Warrior-hero came to Kabûl,
And so set my heart on fire with his love,
That the world became contracted in my sight,
And day and night I wept continually.
I wish not for life except in his presence:
One hair of his head is worth the whole world to me!
When at last he saw and conversed with me,
We joined hand in hand and plighted our faith,
But, beyond seeing and conversing with one another,
The fire of passion hath not inflamed us.
A messenger was sent to the mighty Sâm,
And he returned an answer to the brave Zâl.
For a time the chief was distressed and reluctant,
But he spoke and heard all that was needful;
And after consulting the aged Mubid,
At last he yielded and gave his consent.
To the messenger he gave many presents,
And I also heard all the answers of Sâm.
The woman whose hair thou didst rend,
Whom thou didst strike to the ground, and whose
        face thou didst lacerate,
Was the messenger who was the bearer of the letter;

And this dress was my answer to the message.

Sindocht was confused at her daughter's words,
And in her heart approved of her union with Zâl.
She replied,—Here, indeed, there is nothing of
        littleness!
Amongst the illustrious there is not a Hero like Zâl;
He is mighty, and the son of the warrior of the world;
Wise, and prudent, and of a noble soul.
All excellencies are his, and but one defect,
And, compared with his excellencies, those of others
        are mean.
But I fear that the King of the earth will be enraged
        with him,
And will raise the dust of Kabûl to the sun,
For never will he suffer one of our seed on earth
To place his foot in the stirrup.

To the interview between the mother and daughter
succeeds one between the wife and the husband.

King Mihrab came joyful from the royal reception-
        hall,
For Zâl had bestowed on him much attention.
He beheld lying down the illustrious Sindocht,
Her face pale, and her heart troubled :
And he said to her,—What ailest thou ?
And wherefore are the roses of thy cheeks faded ?

And Sindocht answered and said,
My heart is disturbed with many cares,
This collection of treasures and property,
These Arabian horses trained and caparisoned,
This palace and its surrounding gardens,
This abundance of heart-attached friends,
This band of servants devoted to their master,
This diadem and this imperial throne,
Our commanding presence and lofty dignity,
And all our reputation for wisdom and knowledge,
The fair face of our tall and elegant cypress (*her daughter*),
All our splendour and all our royalty,
By little and little are dwindling away;
Unwillingly we must resign them to an enemy,
And count all our care and painstaking but as wind.
One narrow chest will now suffice us.
The tree which should have been the antidote is become the poison:
We planted, cultivated, and watered it with care;
We hung a crown and jewels on its branches; (*Note 7*)
But when it had raised itself to the sun, and expanded its shade,
It fell to the ground, and my life-stock with it.
Such is the limit and end of our being,
Nor know I where we can find our rest.

D

And Mihrab said to Sindocht,
Thou hast only brought up anew the old story.
This transitory inn is after this fashion ;
One is neglected, and another enjoyeth every comfort ;
One arriveth and another departeth,
And whom see'st thou that Fate hunteth not down ?
By anxiety of heart thou wilt never drive sorrow to
        the door ;
There is no contending with the just God.

Then said Sindocht,—How can I conceal from thee
This secret and these weighty matters ?
Know then that the son of Sâm
Hath secretly ensnared the affections of Rudabah.
He hath led her noble soul astray from the right path ;
And now nothing remaineth for us but to find some
        remedy.
Much counsel have I given her, but it availeth no-
        thing ;
I see her still pale-faced and dejected,
Her heart still full of pain and sorrow,
Her parched lips ever breathing the cold sigh.

When Mihrab heard this, he leaped to his feet ;
He laid his hand on the hilt of his sword,
His body trembled, and his face became livid,

His bosom filled with wrath, and his lips with deep
    groans :
This instant, he exclaimed, the blood of Rudabah
I will pour out like a river on the ground.

When Sindocht saw this, she sprang to her feet,
She seized the belt round his body with both her
    hands,
And exclaimed,—Hear one word ;
Give ear one moment to thine inferiour ;
And afterwards do as thy reason telleth thee,
As thy heart and thy guiding wisdom shall prompt
    thee.

He writhed and flung her from him,
He uttered a cry like a furious elephant ;
And exclaimed,—When a daughter made her appear-
    ance,
I ought to have instantly commanded her to be slain!
I killed her not ; I walked not in the way of my
    ancestors,
And this now is the trick that she hath played me.
But him who departeth from the way of his fathers
The brave will not account to have sprung from his
    loins.
If the Hero Sâm shall join with King Manuchahar,

And they prove their power against me in war,
The smoke will go up from Kabûl to the sun,
Neither dwelling will be left, nor corn-field, nor voice
    of salutation.

Sindocht replied,—O defender of the Marches,
Let not thy tongue utter such wild words,
For the warrior Sâm is already informed of this
    affair ;
Banish from thy mind this terror, and disquiet, and
    anxiety.
Mihrab rejoined—O my mildly-radiant beauty,
Say not a word that is spoken deceitfully ;
My bosom would be free from trouble,
If I saw thee secure from injury.
Than Zâl a son-in-law more estimable
There could not be either amongst the princes or the
    people :
Who might not desire the alliance of Sâm,
From Ahwâz even to Kandahar!

Sindocht answered,—O exalted chief,
What occasion for deceitful words ?
Thy injury is plainly my injury,
And thy troubled soul is bound up in mine ;
Therefore didst thou see me so troubled also,

Sunk down in grief, and all joy gone from my heart!
But should this come about, why would it be so
       wonderful,
That thou shouldest take so dark a view of it?
Feridun approved of the maidens of Yaman,
And this Hero, who seeks to subdue the world, but
       followeth the same path;
For from fire, and water, and earth, and air,
The dark face of the ground is changed to brightness.

Mihrab gave ear to the words of Sindocht,
But his head was still full of vengeful thoughts,
And his heart still boiled over with passion.
Then he gave his commands to Sindocht,
Rouse up and bring Rudabah before me.

But Sindocht was afraid of the lion-hearted man,
Lest he should strike Rudabah to the earth,
First, she said, thou shalt give me a promise,
That thou wilt restore her unhurt to my arms;
And that that heavenly flower shall not be swept
       away from the garden,
And the land of Kabûl be emptied of its roses.
Thou shalt take first a solemn oath,
That thou hast washed out vengeance from thine
       heart.

The warrior gave his word,
That Rudabah should suffer no harm :
But—he said—consider that the Master of the earth,
Will be full of indignation at what hath been done,
And that neither father, nor mother, nor home will be
          left,
And that Rudabah herself will perish in a river of
          blood.

When Sindocht heard this she bowed down her head,
And placed her face on the ground ;
And came to her daughter with smiles upon her lips,
And a face open as the dawn when it riseth on the
          night.
She told her the good news, and said,—The furious
          tiger
Hath withdrawn its grasp from the wild ass.
The hero Mihrab hath sworn by the righteous God
A strong oath, and hath set his name thereto,
That he will not touch in anger a braid of thine hair.
Now therefore bring forth quickly all thine orna-
          ments,
And shew thyself before thy father, and lament what
          hath happened.
But why, said Rudabah, with all my ornaments ?
Why place the valuable beside the valueless ?

My soul is wedded to the son of Sâm,
And why conceal what is so clear?

She appeared before her father like the rising sun,
Immersed in a blaze of gold and rubies;
A charming angel from the realms of Paradise,
Or a glorious sun in the smiling spring.
When her father beheld her he stood fixed in astonish-
       ment,
And secretly invoked the Creator of the world.
O thou, he exclaimed, who hast washed out reason
       from thy brain,
How is this fulness of jewelry beseeming thee!
Is it befitting that a Peri unite herself with Aherman
       (the Evil principle) ?
Rather let my crown and my ring perish!
If a serpent-charmer from the desert of Khoten
       should shew himself as a magician,
Would it not be right to slay him with an arrow?

When Rudabah heard these words her heart burnt
       within her,
And her face was crimsoned with shame in the sight
       of her father;
Her dark eye-lids fell over her grief-swollen eyes,
She stood motionless, and drew not a breath.

Filled, heart and head, with hostility and passion,
Her father groaned in his rage like a roaring tiger.
Rudabah returned heart-broken to the house,
Her pale-yellow cheek alternating with red,
And mother and daughter sought refuge with God.

Meanwhile information of what has happened
reaches the ear of Manuchahar. He is greatly disturbed by it, and sends to summon Sâm to his court.
Sâm obeys the summons, and is received by the King
with great distinction. He is commanded to relate
the history of his wars in Mazinderan, and in answer
to the inquiries of the monarch about his battle with
the Dives, or Demon-inhabitants of the country, he
replies,—
O king, live prosperously for ever !
Far be from thee the designs of the evil-minded !
I came to that city of warlike Dives,
Dives !—rather ferocious lions !
They are fleeter than Arabian horses,
More courageous than the warriors of Irân ;
Their soldiers whom they name Sagsar (*Dog-heads*),
You would think were tigers of war.

When the news of my arrival reached them,
And they heard my shout, their brains were bereft of
             reason ;

They raised a tremendous clamour in their city,
And issued forth in mass,
And collected an army so immense,
That the dust thereof obscured the brightness of the
   day.
Then they rushed towards me, seeking the battle,
Like men insane hurrying and in confusion.
The ground trembled, and the sky was darkened,
As they filled the hills and the valleys.

A panic fell upon my army,
And I could not but be filled with anxiety,
At the serious turn which matters had taken;
But I shouted aloud to my dispirited soldiers,
And raised my ponderous club,
And urged forward my iron-hard charger.
Then I came and clove the heads of the enemy,
So that from dread of me they lost their reason;
At each assault I struck down a hundred bodies,
At every blow of my mace I made a Dive rub the
   ground;
Like feeble deer before the strong lion
They fled affrighted at the ox-headed club.

An aspiring grandson of the bold Salm
Came on like a wolf to meet me in the battle;

The name of the ambitious chieftain was Kâkavi,
Beautiful of countenance, and tall as a cypress.
By his mother he was of the race of Zohâk :
The heads of proud warriors were as dust before him :
His army was as a host of ants or locusts :
Its multitude concealed the plain and the slopes of
    the mountains.
When the dust arose from the approaching squadrons,
The cheeks of our soldiers turned pale ;
But I raised my death-dealing mace, and urged them
    forward,
And led them onward to meet the enemy ;
I shouted so loud from the saddle of my war-horse,
That the earth seemed to whirl like a mill about
    them ;
Courage resumed its place in the breasts of our
    warriors,
And with one determination they rushed to the battle.

When Kâkavi heard my voice,
And saw the wounds of my head-smashing club,
He came to meet me like a mad elephant, seeking to
    wound me.
He desired to entangle me with his long noose ;
But when I saw him I leaped out of way of destruc-
    tion,

And grasping my Kaianian bow,
And selecting my choicest steel-pointed arrows,
I darted them upon him like swift eagles,
And poured them upon him like fiery rain ;
His head, massive as an anvil,
I thought to have nailed to his helmet.
When I saw him through the dust,
Coming on like a mad elephant, his Indian sword in
        his hand,
It came into my mind, O King,
That the very hills were about to ask grace for their
        lives.
He in haste, and I slowly,
I pondered how I might take him in my grasp ;
And when the warrior rushed down upon me,
I stretched out my arm from my war-horse,
Seized the courageous hero by the belt,
Lifted him up lion-like from the saddle,
And furious as an elephant dashed him to the ground,
So that his bones were crushed to atoms.

When their commander was thus laid low,
His army turned back from the field of battle :
On every side they crowded in bands,
Filling the heights and the slopes, the plains and the
        mountains.

When we numbered the slain, horse and foot,
We counted twelve thousand, who had fallen in the
    field ;
The soldiers, and town's-people, and valiant horsemen
Amounted to thirty hundred thousands.
What weight hath the power of the evil-minded
Against thy fortune and the servants of thy throne ?

When Sâm had finished his narrative, Manuchahar
commands him to assemble an army, to march against
Mihrab, to devastate his country, and extirpate his
family. Sâm dares not disobey, and sets off to
execute his commission. On the way he encounters
his son, who earnestly implores him to suspend his
purpose and permit him to go, and himself urge his
suit before the King. Sâm consents and seconds his
request in a letter to Manuchahar, in which he re-
counts his services, and in particular that of having
slain a terrible Dragon which had long desolated the
country.

If I had not appeared in the land,
The heads would have been cut off even of those who
    bear them the highest,
When the huge Dragon came up from the river
    Kashaf,
And made the ground bare as the palm of my hand.

His length was as the distance from city to city,
His breadth as the space from mountain to mountain.
He filled the hearts of all men with terror,
And kept them all on the watch night and day.

I looked, and saw not a bird in the air,
Nor a beast of prey on the face of the ground ;
His flames burnt the feathers of the vulture,
The grass withered beneath his poison,
He drew the fierce water-serpent up from its waters,
And the soaring eagle down from its clouds ;
The earth was emptied of man and beast,
And every thing abandoned its habitation to him.

When I saw that there was no one in the land,
Who was able to crush him with the strong hand,
Relying on the power of the Sovereign of the world,
God the Pure, I cast all fear from my heart,
I girded my loins in the name of the Most High,
I vaulted into the saddle of my massive war-horse,
Grasped in my hand the ox-headed mace,
And, my bow on my arm, and my shield at its neck,
Rushed forward like a furious crocodile,
I with the strong wrist, he with his venom :
And each one who saw by the mace that I was about
            to encounter the Dragon,
Exclaimed to me as I passed,—" Farewell."

I came, I beheld him, huge as a mountain,
Trailing his cord-like hairs upon the ground.
His tongue resembled the black-tree *(the upas ?)*
His jaws open and stretched out on the way.
His two eyes were like two basins of blood ;
He saw me, roared, and sprang upon me with fury :
I thought, O King, so it appeared to me,
That his inside must be filled with fire.
The world appeared to my eyes like an agitated
   ocean ;
A black smoke went-up darkly to the clouds,
The face of the earth trembled at his cry,
From the venom the ground was like the sea of China.
But, as was becoming a valiant man,
I shouted with the voice of a lion,
Placed without delay in my long cross-bow
A choice poplar arrow pointed with adamant,
Aimed the shaft right at his jaws,
That I might nail his tongue to his palate ;
I pierced it on one side with the arrow,
And he lolled it out in utter bewilderment.
In an instant another arrow like the first
I aimed at his mouth, and he writhed from the wound.
A third time I struck him in the midst of his jaws,
And the boiling blood rushed from his vitals.
But, as he narrowed the ground before me,

I upraised the vengeful ox-headed mace,
In the strength of God, the Master of the Universe,
Urged on my elephant-bodied charger,
And battered him in such wise with its blows,
That you would say the sky was raining down moun-
      tains upon him.
I pounded his head as though it was the head of a
      mad elephant,
And from his body streamed the poison like the river
      Nile;
Such was the wound that he never rose again,
And the plain was levelled to the hills with his
      brains;
The river Kashaf became a river of bile,
But the earth was once more an abode of sleep and
      quiet;
And the hills were covered with men and women,
Who called down blessings upon me.

    Zâl arrives at the court of Manuchahar. The king
is highly pleased with his appearance and the proofs
which he gives of his wisdom and courage; but his
fears still make him hesitate to grant his request, and
it is not till he has consulted the astrologers, and
received from them a favourable answer, that he
sanctions it with his approval. Zâl then returns

joyously to Cabûl to communicate the glad tidings to Rudabah.   The nuptials are celebrated with great pomp, and the offspring of the marriage is the Hero Rustam—the Hercules of Persia—whose deeds and adventures fill many subsequent pages of the Shah-namah.

§ *4th.—Miscellaneous Extracts from the Shah-Namah.*

The Death of Dara (Darius).

The Viziers came to Iskandar and said :
" O King, crowned with victories and knowledge,
We have just slain thine enemy.
Come to an end is his diadem and the throne of
    princes."
When Janusyar had thus spoken, Iskandar said to
    Mahyar,
" The enemy ye have cast down—where is he? Shew
    me the nearest road thither."
They went before him, and the King of the Greeks
    followed,
His heart and his eyes filled with tears of blood.
When he came near, he saw that the face of Dara
Was pale as the flower of the fenugreek,
And his breast clotted with gore.

Having commanded that they should quit their horses
And keep guard over the two ministers,
Swift as the wind Iskandar dismounted from his
    charger,
And placed on his thigh the head of the wounded man.
He looked to see whether Dara was still in a condition
    to speak,
Passed both his hands over his face,
Withdrew the royal diadem from his head,
Unclasped the warlike breastplate from his breast,
And rained down a flood of tears from his eyes, when
    he saw the wounded body,
And the physician far away.
May it go well with thee, he exclaimed,
And let the heart of the malevolent tremble !
Raise thyself, and seat thyself on this golden cushion,
And, if thou hast strength enough, place thyself in
    the saddle.
I will bring physicians from Greece and India ;
I will shed tears of blood for thy sufferings ;
I will restore to thee thy kingdom and thy throne,
And we will depart as soon as thou art better.
When, yester-evening, the old men told me what had
    happened,
My heart swelled with blood, my lips uttered cries.
We are of one branch, one root, one body-garment.

Why through our ambition should we extirpate our
　　race ?"—*(Note 8)*

When Dara heard, with a weak voice he replied :

May wisdom be thy companion for ever !

I believe that from thy God—the just, the holy,

Thou wilt receive a recompense for these thy words.

But for what thou hast said, that Persia shall be
　　thine ;

Thine be the throne and the crown of the brave,

Nearer to me is death than a throne ;

My fortune is turned upside down ; my throne is at
　　an end.

Such is the determination of the lofty sphere ;

Its delights are sorrows, and its profit is ruin.

Take heed that thou say not in the pride of thy
　　valour

I have been superiour to this renowned army.

Know that good and evil are alike from God,

And give him the praise that thyself art still alive.

I am, myself, a sufficient example of this ;

And my history is a commentary upon it for every
　　one.

For what greatness was mine and sovereignty, and
　　treasure ;

And to no one hath suffering ever come through me.

What arms and armies too were mine !

And what quantities of horses, and thrones, and
    diadems !
What children and relatives ;
Relatives whose hearts were stamped with my mark.
The earth and the age were as slaves before me ;
So was it as long as fortune was my friend ;
But now I am severed from all my happiness,
And am fallen into the hands of murderers.
I am in despair about my children and my kinsmen ;
The world is become black, and my eyes are darkened.
No one of my relatives cometh to my assistance ;
I have no hope but in the Great Provider, and that
    is enough.
Behold me wounded and stretched upon the ground !
Fate hath ensnared me in the net of destruction.
This is the way of the changeful sphere
With every one, whether he be king or warrior.
In the end all greatness passeth away :
It is a chase in which man is the quarry, and death is
    the hunter.

Iskandar rained tears of anguish from his eyes over
    the wounded King,
As he lay stretched upon the ground.
When Dara perceived that the grief was from his
    heart,

And saw the torrent of tears which flowed from his
        pale cheek,
He said to him,—All this is of no avail :
From the fire no portion is mine but the smoke ;
This is my gift from the All-giver,
And all that remaineth of my once brilliant fortune.
Now give me thine ear from first to last :
Receive what I say, and execute it with judgment.
Iskandar replied, It is for thee to command :
Say what thou wilt, thou hast my promise.

Rapidly Dara unbound his tongue ;
Point by point he gave instructions about everything.
First, illustrious Prince, fear thou God, the Righteous
        Maker,
Who made heaven and earth and time ; who created
        the weak and the strong.
Watch over my children and my kindred, and my
        beloved veiled women.
Ask of me in marriage my chaste daughter, and make
        her happy in thy palace :
To whom her mother gave the name of Roshank,
And in her made the world contented and joyful.
Thou wilt never from my child hear a word of chiding,
Nor will her worst enemy utter a calumny against
        her.

As she is the daughter of a line of kings,

So in prudence she is the crown of women.

Perhaps she will bring thee an illustrious son,

Who will revive the name of Isfandyar,

Will stir up the fire of Zoroaster,

Take in his hand the Zendavesta,

Will observe the auguries and feast of Sadah, and
          that of the new year,

Renew the splendour of the fire temples of Hormuzd,

The Sun, the Moon, and Mithra;

Will wash his face and his soul in the waters of
          wisdom,

Re-establish the customs of Lohrasp,

Restore the Kaianian rites of Gushtasp,

Will treat the great as great and the little as little,

Rekindle religion, and be fortunate.

Iskandar answered,— O good hearted and righteous
          King,

I accept thy injunctions and thy testament.

I will remain in this country only to execute them.

I will perform thy excellent intentions ;

I will make thine intelligence my guide.

The Master of the World seized the hand of Iskandar,

And wept and lamented bitterly.

He placed the palm of it on his lips, and said to him—
    Be God thy refuge!
I leave thee my throne, and return to the dust.
My soul I leave to God the Holy.

He spoke and his soul quitted his body,
And all who were about him wept bitterly.
Iskandar rent all his garments,
And scattered dust on the crown of the Kaianians.
He built a tomb for him agreeably to the customs of
    his country,
And suitable to his faith and the splendour of his
    rank.
They washed the blood from his body with precious
    rose-water,
Since the time of the eternal sleep had arrived.
They wrapped it in brocade of Rûm,
Its surface covered with jewels on a ground of gold.
They hid it under a coating of camphor,
And after that no one saw the face of Dara any more.
In the tomb they placed for him a dais of gold,
And on his head a crown of musk.
They laid him in a coffin of gold,
And rained over him from their eyelids a shower of
    blood.
When they raised the coffin from the ground,

They bore it, turn by turn.

Iskandar went before it on foot,

And the grandees followed behind shedding tears of
        anguish.

So they proceeded to the sepulchre of Dara,

And placed the coffin on the dais, performing all the
        ceremony due to kings ;

And when they had completed the magnificent monu-
        ment,

They erected gibbets before it, and executed the
        murderers.

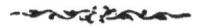

Iskandar's Conversation with the Brahmins.

Iskandar asked the Brahmins about their sleep and
    their food,
How they enjoyed their days of tranquillity, and how
    they supported the dust of the battle.
What is your portion of the delights of the world,
For Fortune never separateth the poison and the
    antidote ?

One of the sages replied :—O conqueror of the world,
No one speaketh here of fame or of battle.
We have no wants as to clothing, reposing, or eating.
Since man cometh naked from his mother,
He ought not to be very delicate in the matter of
    raiment.
Hence he will return naked to the earth,
And here he will find a place of fear, and of sickness,
    and of anxiety.
The ground is our bed, and our covering the sky,
And our eyes are set upon the road,
Waiting for that which time may bring with it.
The ambitious man laboureth excessively for some-
    thing

Which after all is little worth the labour;
For when he leaveth this temporary place of refuge,
He must leave behind him also his crown and his
        treasures.
His sole companions will be his good deeds,
And he and all that he hath will return to the dust.

One of the Brahmins said to him :—O monarch,
Close thou for us the door of death.

He replied :—With Death, vain are all petitions!
What rescue can there be from the sharp claws of that
        dragon ?
For wert thou of iron, from them thou couldest not
        escape.
Youthful as he may be, he who remaineth long here
Will from old age find no deliverance.

The Brahmin answered :—Then, King,
Puissant, and learned, and worthy of empire,
Since thou knowest that for death there is no remedy,
And that there is no worse affliction than old age,
Why give thyself so much pains to win the world ?
Why madly persevere to smell its poisoned flower ?
The misery thou hast caused will remain after thee:
The fruits of thy trouble and thy treasure will go to
        thine enemies.

Nushirvan's Address to the Grandees of Iran.

Leave not the business of to-day to be done to-morrow,
For who knoweth what to-morrow may be thy condition?
The rose garden which to-day is full of flowers,
When to-morrow thou wouldest pluck a rose, may not
afford thee one.
When thou findest thy body vigorous,
Then think of sickness, and pain, and infirmity.
Remember that after life cometh the day of death;
And that before death we are as leaves before the
wind.
Whenever thou enterest on a matter sluggishly,
Thou wilt execute it feebly.
If thou sufferest passion to get the mastery over
prudence,
Thou wilt need no witness to attest thy folly.
The man who talketh much and never acteth
Will not be held in reputation by any one.
By crookedness thou wilt render thy paths the
darker,

But the road towards rectitude is a narrow one.
Even a matter in which thou hast pre-eminent ability
      will turn to evil,
If thou doest it with dulness and inactivity.
If thy tongue allieth itself with falsehood,
No splendour from the throne of heaven will reach
      thee.
A crooked word is the resort of weakness,
And over the weak we can only weep.
If the king rouseth himself from sleep to mount his
      throne,
He will enjoy sound health, and be safe from his
      enemy.
The prudent man will abstain from luxurious living,
And all that goes beyond our actual needs proceedeth
      from greediness,
And is full of pain and anxiety.
If the king is endowed with justice and liberality,
The world will be full of ornament and beauty;
But if crookedness enter into his counsels,
His meat will be the bitter gourd, and his water will
      be blood.

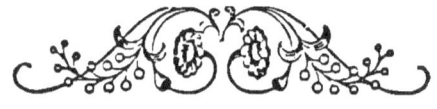

From Nushirvan's Letter to his son Hormuz.

I have thought it meet to write this serious letter to
      my child,
Full of knowledge, and true in the faith;
May God give him happiness, and a prosperous
      fortune!
May the crown and throne of empire be his in per-
      petuity!
In a fortunate month, and on a day of Khurdad (*light
      giving*),
Under a happy star and brilliant omens,
We have placed on thine head a crown of gold,
As we in like manner received it from our father.
And we remember the blessing which the happy
      Kobad
Conferred on our crown and throne.
Be thou vigilant; be master of the world; be
      intelligent;
Be thou of a generous disposition, and do harm to no
      one.

Increase thy knowledge, and attach thyself to God ;
And may He be the guide to thy soul.
I inquired of a man whose words were excellent,
And who was mature in years and in intellect,
Who amongst us is the nearest to God ?
Whose path towards him is the clearest ?
He replied : Chuse knowledge,
If thou desirest a blessing from the Universal-pro-
        vider :
For the ignorant man cannot raise himself above the
        earth ;
And it is by knowledge that thou must render thy
        soul praiseworthy.
It is by knowledge that the king becometh the orna-
        ment of his throne :
Gain knowledge, therefore, and be thy throne vic-
        torious !
Beware thou become not a promise-breaker ;
For the shroud of the promise-breaker will be the
        dust.
Be not a punisher of those who are innocent ;
Lend not thine ear to the words of informers.
In all thy business let thine orders be strictly just ;
For it is by justice that thy soul will be rendered
        cheerful.
Let thy tongue have no concern with a lie,

If thou desirest that thou shouldst reflect a splendour
      on thy throne.
If any one of thy subjects accumulate a fortune,
Preserve him from anxiety about his treasure,
For to take aught from his treasure is to be the enemy
      of thine own :
Rejoice in that treasure which thou hast gained by
      thine own care.
If thy subject shall have amassed wealth,
The monarch ought to be his sustainer ;
Every one ought to feel secure in thine asylum,
However exalted he may be, or however humble.
Whoever doeth thee a kindness, do him the same ;
Whoever is the enemy of thy friend, with him do
      battle.
And if thou comest to honour in the world,
Bethink thee of pains of body, and sorrow, and
      calamity.
Wheresoever thou art, it is but a halting-place ;
Thou must not feel secure, when thou sittest down in it.
Seek, then, to be deserving ; and seat thyself among
      the wise,
If thou desirest the favours of fortune.
When thou placest on thine head the diadem of
      sovereignty,
Seek ever the better way beyond that which is good.

Be charitable to the wretched ; keep thyself far from
    all that is bad ;
And fear for the calamity which thou permittest.
Sound the secret places of thine own heart,
And never show a magnanimity or justice which is
    only on the surface.
Measure thy favours according to merit ;
And listen to the counsels of those who have seen the
    world.
Be inclined to religion, but keep thine eye on the
    Faiths,
For from the Faiths proceed jealousies and anger
    amongst men.
Manage thy treasury in proportion to thy treasure ;
And give thine heart no anxiety about its increase.
Regard the actions of former kings,
And take heed that thou be never otherwise than just.
Where are now the diadems of those Kings of kings ?
Where are those princes, those great ones so favoured
    by fortune ?
Of their acts they have left nothiug behind them but
    the memory :
That is all ; for this transient resting-place remaineth
    to no one.
Give not command recklessly to spill blood,
Nor lightly engage thine army in war.

Walk in the ways of the Lord of sun and moon,
And hold thyself afar from the works of demons.
Keep this letter before thee night and day,
And sound reason perpetually in thine heart.
If thou doest in the world what deserveth remem-
       brance,
Thy name will not perish for lack of greatness.
The Lord of goodness be ever thy refuge;
May earth and time be ever favourable to thee;
May sorrow have no dominion over thy soul;
Aud may the hand of cheerfulness for thee never be
       shortened!
May fortune be ever thy slave;
And may the heads of those who wish evil to thee be
       abased;
May the star of thy destiny ascend to the ninth
       heaven;
And may the Moon and Jupiter be the protectors of
       thy throne;
May the world be irradiated from the splendour of
       thy crown;
And may kings be servants in thy court!
When he had written this letter, he consigned it to
       his treasury,
And continued to live in this transitory world in fear
       and trembling.

Extracts from the Mubid's questions to Nushirvan, and his replies.   (Children and Kindred.)

He said to him : " What is the pleasure of having
    children ?
And why desire to have a family ?"
He gave answer : " He who leaveth the world to his
    children,
Will not himself be forgotten.
When he hath children life has a savour,
And its savour will keep vice at a distance ;
And, when he is passing away, his pangs will be
    lessened,
If a child be looking on his paling countenance.
Even he who liveth to do good will pass away,
And time will count out his respirations."
" Wherefore, then," he said, " praise virtue,
Since Death cometh and moweth down alike the good
    and the evil ?"
He replied : " Good deeds

Will obtain their full value in every place :
The man who died doing good actions is not dead ;
He is at rest and hath consigned his soul to God :
But he is not at rest who remaineth behind,
And leaveth in the world a bad report."
The Mubid said :—" Of evil things there is nothing
       worse than death ;
How can we make provision against that ?"
He answered him :—" When thou passest away from
       this sombre earth,
Thou wilt find a brighter abode ;
But he who hath lived in fears and remorse,
Is compelled to weep over a life so spent.
Whether thou be king, or whether thou be of the low-
       born,
Thou wilt have passed away from the terrors and the
       sorrows of the world."
He said : " Of these two things which is the worst,
And which will cause us the greatest pain and unhap-
       piness ?"
He replied : " Be assured that nothing will press upon
       thee with the weight of a mountain
If it come as a multitude, like Remorse.
In the world there is nothing so strong as Remorse !
What terror is there, if it be not the terror of
       Remorse ?"

(Destiny.)

The Mubid asked :—" What are we to think of the
  action of the heavenly sphere ?"
Interpret to me its revelations and its mysteries.
Are we to accept and approve its operations,
Even if its mutations bring with them what seems
  not salutary ?
He gave answer :—" This aged sphere,
Though it is charged with knowledge and memories;
Though it is great, and powerful, and loftier than
  aught else,
And though it is lord above all lords,
Follow not thou its ordinances, nor approve them;
Look not to it for advantage or disadvantage.
Know that evil and good are from Him that hath no
  partner ;
Whose operations have no beginning and have no
  end.
When He says BE ! it is done to His hand;
He Was, and ever was; and Is, and ever Is."

(How we may best serve God.)

Seat thyself always in the society of the wise;
And strive after those enjoyments which are eternal;
For earthly enjoyments will pass away,
And the wise man will not reckon them enjoyments.
Incline thine affections to learning and knowledge,
For these must show thee thy way towards God.
Do not let thy words go beyond measure;
For thou art but a young creature, and the world is
     old.
Suffer not thyself to be intoxicated by the revolutions
     of fortune,
And let thy companionship not be with evil men.
Tear away thine heart from that which cannot be,
And bestow all that it is in thy power to bestow.
Withhold not whatsoever thou hast from a friend,
Even if he ask for thine eye, thy brain, or thy skin.
If a friend would settle an account with a friend,
Let him not admit an intermediate in the matter.
If thou must have intercourse with an evil-minded
     man,
Give him no opportunity of laying his hand upon
     thee.

If any one would open the path of intimacy,

Take care that he is a man of virtue, and modesty,
      and gentleness.

Let not thy tongue go beyond thy merits,

For the just man will not number false pretences as
      merits.

He will not hold any one great for his possessions;

Nor, on the other hand, esteem any one mean for his
      poverty.

The Raja of India sends a Chessboard to Nushirvan.

When this heart-absorbing question was brought to
 an end,
My narrative must proceed to the subject of Chess.—
      (Note 9.)
A Mubid related, how one day the King
Suspended his crown over the ivory throne,
All aloes-wood and ivory, and all ivory and aloes,
Every pavilion a court, and every court a royal one,
All the Hall of Audience crowned with soldiers,
Every pavilion filled with Mubids and Wardens of the
     Marches,
From Balkh, and Bokhara, and from every frontier,
For the King of the World had received advices
From his vigilant and active emissaries,
That an Ambassador had arrived from a King of
   India,
With the Parasol, and elephants, and cavalry of Sind,
And accompanied by a thousand laden camels,
Was on his way to visit the Great King.

When the circumspect Monarch heard this news,
Immediately he despatched an escort to receive him ;
And when the illustrious and dignified Ambassador
Came into the presence of the Great King,
According to the manner of the great he pronounced
          a benediction,
And uttered the praise of the Creator of the world.
Then he scattered before him abundance of jewels,
And presented the Parasol, the elephants, and the
          ear-rings ;
The Indian Parasol embroidered with gold,
And inwoven with all kinds of precious stones.
Then he opened the packages in the midst of the
          Court,
And displayed each one, article by article, before the
          King.
Within the chest was much silver, and gold,
And musk, and amber, and fresh wood of aloes,
Of rubies, and diamonds, and Indian swords,
Each Indian sword beautifully damascened ;
Every thing which is produced in Kanûj and Mai,
Hand and foot was busy to put in its place.
They placed the whole together in front of the throne,
And the Chief, the favoured of wakeful fortune,
Surveyed all that the Raja had painstakingly collected,
And then commanded that it should be sent to his
          treasury.

Then the Ambassador presented, written on silk,
The letter which the Raja had addressed to
     Nushirvan ;
And a chessboard wrought with such exceeding
     labour,
That the pains bestowed upon it might have emptied
     a treasury ;
And the Indian delivered a message from the Raja :
" So long as the heavens revolve mayest thou be
     established in thy place.
All who have taken pains to excel in knowledge,
Command to place this chessboard before them,
And to exert their utmost ingenuity
To discover the secret of this noble game.
Let them learn the name of every piece,
Its proper position, and what is its movement.
Let them make out the foot-soldier of the army,
The elephant, the rook, and the horseman,
The march of the Vizier and the procession of the
     King.
If they discover the science of this noble game,
They will have surpassed the most able in science.
Then the tribute and taxes which the King hath
     demanded,
I will cheerfully send all to his Court.
But if the congregated sages, men of Irân,

Should prove themselves completely at fault in this
  science,
Then since they are not strong enough to compete
  with us in knowledge,
Neither should they desire taxes or tribute from this
  land and country.
Rather ought we to receive tribute from you,
Since knowledge hath a title beyond all else."

Khosru gave heart and ear to the speaker,
And impressed on his memory the words which he
  heard.
They placed the chessboard before the King,
Who gazed attentively at the pieces a cosniderable
  time.
Half the pieces on the board were of brilliant ivory,
The other half of finely imaged teak-wood.
The nicely-observant King questioned him much
About the figures of the pieces and the beautiful board.
The Indian said in answer—" O thou great monarch,
All the modes and customs of war thou wilt see,
When thou shalt have found out the way to the
  game ;
The plans, the marches, the array of the battle-field."
He replied,—" I shall require the space of seven days,
On the eighth we will encounter thee with a glad
  mind."

They furnished forthwith a pleasant apartment,
And assigned it to the Ambassador as his dwelling.

Then the Mubid and the skilful to point out the way
Repaired with one purpose to the presence of the
      King.
They placed the chess-board before them,
And observed it attentively time without measure.
They sought out and tried every method,
And played against one another in all possible ways.
One spoke and questioned, and another listened,
But no one succeeded in making out the game.
They departed each one with wrinkles on his brow,
And Buzarchamahar went forthwith to the King.

He perceived that he was ruffled and stern about this
      matter,
And in its beginning foresaw an evil ending.
Then he said to Khosru,—" O Sovereign,
Master of the world, vigilant, and worthy to com-
      mand,
I will reduce to practice this noble game,
All my intelligence will I exert to point out the way."
Then the King said,—" This affair is thine affair,
Go thou about it with a clear mind and a sound body,
Otherwise the Raja of Kanûj would say,

He hath not one man who can search out the road,
And this would bring foul disgrace on my Mubids,
On my Court, on my Throne, and on all my wise
    men.

Then Buzarchamahar made them place the chessboard
        before him,
And seated himself, full of thought, and expanded his
        countenance.
He sought out various ways, and moved the pieces to
        the right hand and to the left,
In order that he might discover the position of every
        piece.
When, after a whole day and a whole night, he had
        found out the game,
He hurried from his own pavilion to that of the King,
And exclaimed,—" O King, whom Fortune crowneth
        with victory,
At last I have made out these figures and this chess-
        board.
By a happy chance, and by the favour of the Ruler
        of the World,
The mystery of this game hath found its solution.
Call before thee the Ambassador and all who care
        about it ;
But the King of kings ought to be the first to behold it.

You would say at once without hesitation,
It is the exact image of a Battle-field."
The King was right glad to hear this news;
He pronounced him the Fortunate, and the bearer of
      good tidings.
He commanded that the Mubids and other Counsellors,
And all who were renowned for their wisdom, should
      be assembled;
And ordered that the Ambassador should be sum-
      moned to the Presence,
And that he should be placed on a splendid throne.

Then Buzarchamahar, addressing him, said,
" O Mubid, bright in council as the sun,
Tell us, what said the King about these pieces,
So may intelligence be coupled with thee for ever!"

And this was his answer,—" My Master, prosperous
      in his undertakings,
When I was summoned and appeared before him,
Said to me,—These pieces of teak and ivory
Place before the throne of him who weareth the
      crown,
And say to him—Assemble thy Mubids and Coun-
      sellors,
And seat them, and place the pieces before them.

If they succeed in making out the noble game,
They will win applause and augment enjoyment:
Then slaves and money, and tribute and taxes,
I will send to him as far as I have the means;
For a monarch is to be esteemed for his wisdom,
Not for his treasure, or his men, or his lofty throne.
But if the King and his counsellors are not able to
     do all this,
And their minds are not bright enough to compre-
     hend it,
He ought not to desire from us tribute or treasure,
And his wise soul, alas! must come to grief;
And when he se'eth our minds and genius to be
     subtler than theirs,
Rather will he send them to us in greater abundance."

Then Buzarchamahar brought the chess-men and
     board,
And placed them before the throne of the watchful
     King,
And said to the Mubids and Counsellors,
" O ye illustrious and pure-hearted sages,
Give ear all of you to the words he hath uttered,
And to the observations of his prudent Chief."

Then the knowing-man arranged a battle-field,
Giving to the King the place in the centre;

Right and left he drew up the army,

Placing the foot-soldiers in front of the battle.

A prudent Vizier he stationed beside the King,

To give him advice on the plan of the engagement ;

On each side he set the elephants of war (*our bishops*),

To support one another in the midst of the combat.

Further on he assigned their position to the war-
steeds (*our knights*),

Placing upon each a horseman eager for the battle.

Lastly, right and left, at the extremities of the field,

He stationed the heroes (*the rooks*) as rivals to each
other.

When Buzarchamahar had thus drawn up the army,

The whole assembly was lost in astonishment,

But the Indian Ambassador was exceedingly grieved,

And stood motionless at the sagacity of that fortune-
favoured man.

Stupefied with amazement, he looked upon him as a
magician,

And his whole soul was absorbed in his reflections.

" For never hath he seen," he said, " a chessboard
before,

Nor ever hath he heard about it from the experienced
men of India.

I have told him nothing of the action of these pieces,

Not a word have I said about this arrangement and
         purpose.
How then hath this revelation come down upon him ?
No one in the world will ever take his place !"

And Khosru was so proud of Buzarchamahar,
Thou mightest say that he was looking Fortune in
         the face.
He was gladdened at his heart and loaded him with
         caresses,
And ordered him a more than ordinary dress of
         honour,
And commanded to be given him a royal cup
Filled to the brim with princely jewels,
And a quantity of money, and a charger and a saddle,
And dismissed him from the Presence overwhelmed
         with praises.

Ardashir's Address to the Nobles of Persia.

When from Greece to China, from Turistan to Hin-
    dustan,
The world had become brilliant as the silk of Rûm,
And tribute and customs had been gathered in from
    every province,
And no one had strength to resist its Lord,
Ardashir called together all the Grandees of Persia,
And seated them according to their ranks on their
    princely thrones.

Then the Master of the World stood up and uttered
    good and righteous words,—
O most illustrious men of your country,
Who have all of you your portion of intelligence and
    wisdom,
Know that the swiftly revolving sphere is not indul-
    gent through justice,
Nor holdeth out its arms through benevolence.

Every one whom it willeth, it exalteth to dignity;

And whomsoever it willeth, it abaseth to the sombre
      dust :

Nothing but his name will remain on the earth,

And all the fruits of his anxiety will pass into
      oblivion.

Strive not then for any thing except a good name,

All ye who hope for a good end.

Turn thou to God !   Open thyself to God !

For He it is who possesseth, and can augment thy
      felicity.

In every evil let the Lord of the Universe be thy
      refuge,

For He it is who hath the power over good and evil.

He can make easy to thee every difficulty :

From Him cometh heart-cheering and victorious
      fortune.

First of all take example from my own affairs ;

Renew the memory of my own past, good and evil.

As soon as I made the Ruler of the World my refuge,

My heart was rejoiced with the crown and royalty ;

And the lands of the seven zones became my kingdom,

As He, in His sovereign authority, judged proper.

Whoever shall offer Him praise worthy of His works,

Perchance his service He will remember,

And shew to him His greatness and His power.

Stretch forth all ye your hands towards God!
Labour and faint not in your compact with Him!
For He is the giver, and He is the possessor,
And He is the painter of the lofty skies.
To him who hath suffered oppression He will bring
assistance.
Glorify not yourselves, any of you, in the face of His
glory.
Let each one beware how he setteth his heart upon
fraud ;
After the rise followeth the descent.

Hold not anyone knowledge in contempt,
Whether he be subject or king ;
For never doth the word of the wise man become old.
The dread of committing a fault is more than the
fetters and prison of the king.
One thing also I will tell you,
Which is higher than aught that you have seen or
thought.
Happy he, who hath made the world happier !
And whose secret acts and open ones are all the same!
Happy, too, he ! who has a soft voice, and an intelli-
gent mind,
And a modest air, and earnest speech.
Watch over thine expenditure, for he who through
vain glory

Spendeth uselessly what he hath on empty follies
Will receive neither return, nor praise from anyone,
Nor the approval of him who serveth God.
If thou chuse the middle way, thou mayst keep
      thy place,
And men of sense will pronounce thee wise.
To pass quietly through the world four paths lie
      before thee,
Which thou mayest tread in piety and faith ;
In which thou mayest increase thy health of body and
      peace of mind,
And taste the honey without the poison.
First, through ambition or avarice, attempt not to go
Beyond what the bounty of the All-giver hath assigned
      thee.
Whoever is contented, he is rich ;
For him the rose-tree of the fresh spring leaveth
      innumerable flowers.
Secondly, court not battles and glory,
For battles and glory bring with them grief and pain.
Thirdly, keep thine heart afar from sorrow,
And be not anxious about the trouble which is not
      yet come.
Fourthly, meddle not in a matter which is not thine:
Pursue not the game which concerneth not thee.

O thou who wouldest penetrate to the marrow of the
    subject,
Break off thy heart from this old hostelry,
For, like you and me, it hath seen many guests,
Nor will it suffer any one long to rest within it.
Whether thou be king, or whether thou be servant,
Thou must pass on, whilst itself remains permanent.
Whether thou be in sorrow, or whether thou be
    enthroned and crowned,
Thou must at a word bind up thy package.
If thou art made of iron, Destiny will wear thee
    down,
And when thou art aged he will not fondle thee.
When the heart-delighting cypress is bowed,
When the sad narcissus is weeping,
When the rosy cheek is saffron,
When the head of the joyous man is heavy,
When the spirit slumbereth, and when what was
    erect is bowed down,
Wouldest thou remain alone, the companions of thy
    journey all departed ?
Whether thou be monarch, or whether thou be subject,
No other resting-place shalt thou have than the dark
    earth.
Where are the mighty ones with their thrones and
    crowns ?

Where are the horsemen elated with victory ?
Where those bold and intelligent warriors ?
Where those valiant and exalted chieftains ?
Their only pallet now is the earth and a few bricks—
Happy, if only they have left a fair fame !

The Last Words of Ardashir to his Son.

The foundation of a king's throne may be shaken in
    three ways.
First, because the king is an unjust one.
Secondly, because he bringeth forward an unprincipled
    man,
And exalteth him above the virtuous one.
Thirdly, when he expendeth his riches on himself,
Or laboureth only to make his treasure more.
Make thyself conspicuous for justice and liberality,
And suffer no false person to come nigh unto thee.
Falsehood darkeneth the countenance of a king;
An evil-minded man will lose all his splendour.
Take heed that thou guard not thy treasure too closely,
For men through money fall into affliction.
Whenever the king is seized with the passion of
    avarice,
He exposeth the bodies of his subjects to suffering.
Exert thyself to keep anger at a distance;

Close thine eye as in sleep to the fault of the misdoer.
If thou yieldest to anger, shame will follow thee.
When he maketh his apology, apply the remedy—
    forgiveness.
When the king abandoneth himself to anger,
The wise man will esteem him of little worth.
Since it is a fault in a king to wish evil to any one,
He should study to fill his heart with kindness.

Such is the action of the revolving sphere;
Sometimes it bringeth pain, and sometimes gladness.
Sometimes fortune is like a vicious horse,
And in the midst of thy prosperity its caprice in-
    volveth thee in misfortune.
At another time it is a charger at full speed,
Tossing its head on high in its good will.
Know, my son, that this palace of deception
Will not permit thee to enjoy thyself without terrors.
Watch over thy body and over thy mind,
If thou desirest that thy day should not turn to evil.
When the king payeth homage to religion,
Religion and royalty are brethren;
Nor can religion be stable without royalty;
Nor can royalty be permanent without religion.
They are two foundations interlaced with one another,
Which intelligence hath combined in one.

Religion cannot do without royalty;
Neither can royalty be maintained without religion.
They are like two sentinels keeping guard over one
        another
Under the same tent *(or cloak)*.
Neither can this one do without that,
Nor can that one do without this:
Thou wouldest say that they are two partners,
Associated for the purpose of doing good.

Leave not till to-morrow the business of to-day;
Nor place upon a throne one who counseleth to evil.
Fear the evil men who contrive evil in secret;
For from bad men who work in secret cometh the
        misery of the world.
Trust not thy secret to a confidant,
For he too will have his associates and friends,
And it will be spread abroad through the whole city;
And men will call thee weak-headed,
And the wise ones will tell thee that anger becometh
        thee not.
In no wise ask about the faults of others,
For he who reporteth the faults of others will report
        thine also:
And if passion gaineth the mastery over reason,
The wise will not count thee amongst men.

The sovereign of the world, who should be benevolent
      to every one,
Ought to be a man of intelligence ;
And, God forbid, that one of sharp and arrogant
      disposition,
Who turneth not away from calumnies and reproaches,
Should take his place beside thee,
Or be a counsellor and guide to thee.
If thou desirest that the pure in heart should praise
      thee,
Lay aside anger and vengeance when thou becomest
      king.
Be not a man of many words,
And parade not thy virtues in the face of others.
Listen to every word, and remember the best ;
And look well before thou takest any one to thine heart.
Weigh well thy words in the presence of the learned;
Shew to every one a courteous demeanour and a
      pleasant countenance.
Treat not with contempt the poor petitioner ;
And seat not the malevolent man upon a throne.
If any one asketh pardon for his fault receive it,
And take not vengeance for a past injury.

Be a just judge and a providence to all :
Happy the man who is generous and patient !

When thine enemy feareth thee, he will use flattering
    words;
But do thou then array thine army, and sound the
    drum,
And throw thyself into the battle,
Till his hand become weak and he retire.
But if he seek peace, and thou see'st that he is sincere,
And that there is no falsehood in his heart,
Take tribute from him, and seek not vengeance,
And have respect to his honour.
Adorn thy mind with knowledge, for knowledge
    maketh thy worth;
And when thou knowest, practice what thou knowest.
If thou art generous thou wilt be beloved;
And with justice and knowledge thou wilt become
    illustrious.

Lay to thy soul the injunctions of thy father,
And preserve them for a memorial to thy children.
When I have left to my children their rightful
    heritage,
I shall have done an injury to no one.
And thou, do not neglect these my injunctions,
And do not for an instant pervert my words.
Turn towards the good, and let the bad be as the wind.

Grieve not my spirit by any perversity, nor my frail
    body with fire.
Employ not thy power, O my son, to do evil to others;
And seek not to pain or afflict any one.

Now I am prepared for my departure :
Commit me to the tomb, and do thou ascend thy
    throne.
I have borne many sorrows in the world;
Some in public, others in secret ;
Gladden my spirit by thy justice, and be victorious
    and joyful on thy throne !

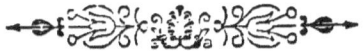

The Gardens of Afrasiab.

See'st thou yonder plain, so red and yellow,
Which might fill the heart of a brave man with delight?
All grove, and garden, and running waters;
A place fit for a Court of Heroes!
The ground pictured silk, and its air fragrant with
  musk;
Thou mightest almost say, that its streamlets were
  rose water.
The stalk of the jasmine bendeth beneath its load,
The rose is the idol, and the nightingale its wor-
  shipper.
The pheasant strutteth about in the midst of flowers;
The turtle-dove cooeth, and the nightingale warbleth
  from the cypress.
From the present moment to the latest times
The banks of its rivulets will resemble Paradise.
Fairy-faced damsels wilt thou see on every hill and
  in every dale,

And seated in gay groups on every side.
There, Manisha, the daughter of Afrasiab,
Maketh the whole garden dazzling as the sun !
There, Sitarah, his second daughter, sitteth in royal
    glory amidst her attendants,
Adorning the plain and eclipsing the rose and the lily !
All veiled and lovely maidens, all tall and elegant as
    the cypress,
All graced with musky ringlets,
All with rosy cheeks and sleepy eyes,
All with ruby lips, and sweet as rose water.
Were we to make a single day's journey,
And rush suddenly on that palace of delights,
We might capture some of those fairy-faced damsels,
And make ourselves precious in the sight of Khosru.

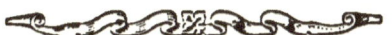

Introduction to the History of Hormuz.

The month Tammuz (*July*) smiled at the red apples,
And sportively rallied the apple-tree about its fruit
    and its leaves.
Where is that nosegay of roses which in the spring-
    tide,
Drunk with joy, thou didst wear in thy bosom?
Which from its colour breathed a hue of modesty,
And from its stalk exhaled a perfume of tenderness,
What hast thou done with it?—Who hath been the
    purchaser of it?
Where didst thou find for it so capital a market?
Who hath given thee in exchange for it those cor-
    nelians and emeralds,
The great weight of which boweth down thy branches?
Assuredly, thou must have asked a good price for thy
    flowers,
And thus adorned thy cheek with those lovely colours!
A hue of bashfulness tingeth thy neck;
Thy garment is scented with a musky fragrance.

Perchance thou hast stolen the sheen of thy robe from
    Jupiter ;
Thy pearls thou hast spotted with drops of blood.
Thy bosom is become emerald, thy skin violet ;
Thine head is more exalted than the standard of
    Kawa (*the standard of Persia*).
With thy garment become russet, and yellow, and
    white,
Thou hast rendered me hopeless of the leaves of thy
    blossom.
O mine idol ! O my spring ! whither art thou gone ?
Why hast thou hidden the ornament of thy garden ?
The autumn still exhibiteth the perfume of thy zephyrs.
In a cup of wine I will renew thy memory.
When thy colours shall have become yellow, I will
    yet praise thee ;
I will still adorn thee as the diadem of Hormuz.
And if to-day my marketing be successful,
Thou shalt yet see traces of me after my death.

Reflections of Ferdusi on Old Age and Death.

What sayeth the ambitious chief of the village, my
　　teacher?
What of the mutations of the revolving spheres?
One day we are climbing, another we are descending;
Now we are cheerful, and now we are in anxiety.
Our end is a pillow upon the dark earth;
For one in high places, for another in a ditch.
We have no token from those who are departed,
Whether they are awake and happy, or whether they
　　are asleep.
In this world, however little of happiness hath been
　　our portion,
Yet have we no desire for death.
Whether thou be'st a hundred years old, or whether
　　thou be'st twenty and five,
It is all one; when the memory cometh to thee of the
　　day of anguish.

Whether he can speak of life as cheerful and delicate,
Or whether he speak of it as full of pain, and anxiety,
    and sorrow,
Never yet have I seen any one who wished to die;
Whether he was one who had strayed out of the right
    way, or whether he was one of virtuous habits.
Whether he was one of the faithful, or whether he
    was an impious adorer of idols,
When Death cometh he will place both hands upon
    his head.
When, old man! thy years shall have passed sixty
    and one,
The cup and the wine and repose 'will have lost their
    savour;
And the man who hath attained sound sense and
    wisdom
Will not attach his heart to this transitory resting
    place.
Of thy friends, many will remain behind, and many
    will have gone before,
And thou, with thy cup, wilt have been left alone in
    the desert.
If thou dost not well consider in the beginning what
    thou hast to do,
Repentance without remedy will be thy portion at the
    end.

Rejoice not, if thou hast done evil;

For thou wilt have injured thyself, if thou shalt have
injured another.

However many years thou mayest still be here,

Know that thy departure will come at last;

Therefore increase in goodness so long as thou art
here,

That when thou departest, in that thou mayest still be
joyful:

According to our words and deeds in this life

Will be hereafter the remembrance of us in the world.

For myself, from the revolution of the spheres I ask
only,

That so much time and so much cheerfulness of spirit
may be left me,

That these histories and these traditions, which have
become ancient,

And over which so many years have passed,

From the time of Kaiumeras (*the first king*) to that of
Yezdejerd (*the last*),

I may connect together and disperse abroad by my
writings;

And may clear this garden of its deforming weeds,

And revive the words and deeds of the king of Kings:

Then will I not grieve to depart,
And abandon this temporary halting-place.

NOTES AND ILLUSTRATIONS.

NOTE 1. PAGE 9.—Other accounts say that this encounter took place, not fortuitously at the entrance of Ferdusi into Ghazni, but in a court or garden of the King's Palace, and in his presence : a kind of competative examination. Probably neither account is much to be trusted as absolutely correct, and is to be received only as an illustration of Oriental ideas and feeling about the Poet.

NOTE 2. PAGE 23.—This is very likely only an approximative estimate. Turner Macan, the learned and laborious editor of the printed edition of the Shah-Namah, in 4 vols., Calcutta, 1829, says in the Preface, vol. 1, page 39—"Ferdusi himself alludes to this number, but it may be doubted if he did not calculate in a loose and general manner, and without having counted the verses. But whatever number of couplets this poem may have originally contained, I have never seen a manuscript with more than fifty-six thousand six hundred and eighty-five, including doubtful and spurious passages. The present edition contains fifty-five thousand two hundred and four, exclusive of the Appendix." It is not wonderful that in so long a work, preserved for so many centuries only in MSS., transcribed by so many hands, and in so widely separated countries, many variations of readings and many omissions and discrepancies should have crept into the copies. Rather it is wonderful that they should have maintained such resemblance as still exists.

Note 3. Page 30.—Preface to Lumsden's edition of Ferdusi, Calcutta, 1811, page 3. This, the first attempt at a printed text of the original, was intended to have been produced in eight volumes folio, and to have comprised the whole of the Shah-Namah. But, though the editor received the patronage and aid of the East India Company, he was unhappily obliged to abandon his task, for which great preparation had been made and under most favourable circumstances, on account of the heavy expense of printing, &c. It may not be unsuitable to mention here, that the

magnificent edition of the Shah-Namah, undertaken
by the late Professor Mohl, at Paris, under royal and
imperial authority, with an elegant translation into
French on the opposite page, which had slowly
reached its fifth volume in folio, is suspended for the
present by the death of its lamented author; whether
with the materials collected for finishing it, and the
intention of doing so, under another editor, is not
known to the writer. The complete edition, in four
octavo volumes, by Turner Macan, is mentioned
in Note 2, above; and some Persian students of the
Shah-Namah may be glad to be informed, that the
writer of this note has now lying before him the first
number of a new edition of the entire work by
Professor J. A. Vuller, to be published, 5s. 4d. the
number. *Lug. Bat. sumptibus E. J. Brill, 1876.*

NOTE 4. PAGE 31.—
So Ovid,
Jamque opus, exegi, &c.
And Horace,
Exegi monumentum ære perennius, &c.
Is there not rather something fine in this proud
consciousness of genius, relying on its own internal
strength, not on the weak and mutable opinion of
others,—in these confident anticipations of immortal
fame, the richest reward of the poet. Who that has

read the pathetic complaint of Camoens, at the end
of the 5th Canto of the Lusiad, does not rejoice to
know that, amidst poverty and neglect, he was yet
cheered with the hope that justice would one day be
done to his injured merit.

NOTE 5.   PAGE 34.—As it may throw light on this
and some other passages, it may, perhaps, not be
unimportant briefly to notice that a great and essential
difference lies between our writers and those of the
East, in the use of comparisons and similitudes.   We
require the thing compared to agree with the object
of comparison in the major part, or, at least, in a
considerable number, of its points; whereas the
Eastern poet seeks only for a single point of
resemblance.   For example : No comparison occurs
more frequently in Persian poetry than that between
a beautiful woman and the moon—a comparison
which, with our ideas, is apt to excite some ludicrous
associations.   Yet it is certain, that no such associations enter into the mind of the Persian poet, who
simply means to ascribe to the countenance of his
mistress the mild radiance and softened lustre, so
beautifully assigned to that planet by Pope, in these
exquisite verses : —

> " So when the sun's broad beam has tire'l the sight,
> All mild ascends the moon's more sober light ;
> Serene in virgin modesty she shines,
> And unobserv'd the glaring orb declines."

In this, and in all similar cases, it would be a good rule for the translator from the Persian to introduce now and then a word which should mark the point of resemblance—" An eye *radiant* as the moon"—" A hero *strong* as an elephant, and *valiant* as a lion." It may just be observed, in passing, that this Oriental use of figures illustrates the application of many parables in the sacred writings—those, for instance, of the " Unjust Steward" and " The Importunate Widow."

Those who wish to obtain more information on this subject will meet with some curious observations in Professor Lumsden's Persian Grammar, vol. 2nd, p. 494.

NOTE 6. PAGE 39.—

> " Should at my feet the world's great master fall.
> Himself, his throne, his world, I'd scorn them all ;
> Not Cæsar's Empress would I deign to prove!
> No! make me mistress to the man I love.
> *Eloisa to Abelard.*

NOTE 7. PAGE 53.—Those who are interested in such inquiries will meet with a curious dissertation on the high respect paid to certain trees in the East, to which allusion may here be made in the appendix to the first volume of Sir William Ouseley's Travels in Persia, pages 359-401.

NOTE 8.   PAGE 71.—According to the Eastern legend, Darab, the predecessor and father of Dara, the Darius of the Greeks, married Nahid, a daughter of Failakas, Philip of Macedon, and was the father of Alexander.   Nahid was on a visit at the Court of her father, when Iskandar, or Alexander, was born. Philip was overjoyed at the event, and having no son of his own, determined to keep it secret, and made Iskandar his heir.   Darab afterwards married a second wife, and was the father of Dara.   Dara and Iskandar, therefore, were, according to the story, half-brothers.

NOTE 9.   PAGE 91.—This account of the game of Chess, written by Ferdusi eight hundred years ago, is curious, as showing the antiquity of the game, its resemblance to it as now played, and the tradition, that it was invented in India, and came originally from that country.

By the same Translator, and published in the same form, at 1s. 6d. each volume, by Williams & Norgate, Henrietta-street, Covent Garden, London; and James Cornish, Piccadilly, Manchester:—

I. Sketch of the Life and Writings of Ferdusi, a Persian Heroic Poet who flourished in the tenth century; with Specimens of the SHAH-NAMAH, or BOOK OF KINGS.

II. Memoir of the Life and Writings of NIZAMI, a Persian Poet who flourished in the twelfth century; with an Analysis of the Second Part of his ALEXANDER BOOK, from the German of Dr. Bacher.

III. Flowers Culled from the GULISTAN or ROSE GARDEN, and from the BOSTAN or PLEASURE GARDEN of SADI, a Persian Moral Poet who flourished in the twelfth century; with a few Specimens of the MESNAVI of JELAL-UD-DIN RUMI.

IV. A CENTURY OF GHAZELS, or a HUNDRED ODES, from the Diwân of HAFIZ, a Persian Lyrical Poet who flourished in the fourteenth century.

V. Analysis and Specimens of JOSEPH AND ZULAIKHA, by JAMI, a Persian Romantic Poet who flourished in the fifteenth century.